MAIL-ORDER BRIDE SURPRISE

MONTANA MAIL-ORDER BRIDES
BOOK TWO

LINDA FORD

1

MONTANA, 1890

*S*he would do whatever was required to achieve her goal.

Honor Ward wound her long braid into a bun at the back of her head and fixed it in place with a dozen hairpins. *Please stay tidy.* She donned a gray bonnet and tied it under her chin. Her friend Tammy had said the hat was appropriate. Honor took her word for it.

She smoothed her dark gray skirt and adjusted the matching jacket. Both showed the signs of travel, and both still felt uncomfortable, but Tammy had insisted they were necessary as were the two dresses she'd given Honor as a going-away present. She owed so much to her friend, not the least of which...

The train jerked to a stop.

"Crow Crossing, Montana." The conductor patted her shoulder. "It's your destination, my dear. May God be with you and grant you your every dream."

"Thank you." The man's words strengthened her resolve.

She picked up her satchel. Tammy had offered to give her one, but Honor had used the last of her meager savings to buy her own. Holding her head high and ignoring the frantic, erratic beat of her heart, she marched down the aisle, prepared to face her unknown future.

She let the conductor assist her from the train and stood on the wooden platform, trying to take it all in at once. A woman and child hurried away. A porter unloaded luggage from the freight car. Her own trunk was placed on a trolley.

Steam and smoke came from the train. As she turned her head, she caught a whiff of untainted air and she breathed deeply. Her full lungs did little to ease her sudden bout of nerves. *I can do this. It's what I want. Everything will be all right once we've met.*

She shifted her attention to the wooden platform. A man crossed toward her. Was it him? Twenty-four years old, his letters had said. He was of a good height. From what she could see under his brown cowboy hat, his hair was dark blond though he'd described it as light brown.

He took two steps toward her. "Miss Ward? Honor Ward?"

It was him!

She stared, trying to take in every detail. He was pleasant looking. His eyes were steady though she couldn't make out their color.

She swallowed hard before she could speak. "Mr. Shannon, I presume."

"Luke Shannon."

She took a step toward him and wobbled in the fashionable shoes Tammy had insisted were appropriate. She should have worn her comfortable, sturdy boots. Her ankle twisted and she tumbled forward.

Mr. Shannon—Luke—caught her before she fell on her face.

This was not the way she'd meant to greet him. But she clung to his arms, his steady grasp was most welcome. He'd said his eyes were light brown, but they were almost golden in color though perhaps the sunlight made them appear so. Or her own sudden dizziness.

She straightened and made sure she was well-balanced. "Forgive my clumsiness."

He chuckled. "No need to fall at my feet."

His humor tickled her, and she laughed. "I'll bear that in mind in the future."

They regarded each other. A number of letters had gone back and forth but seeing him for the first time was a different matter. She liked what she saw. Would he feel the same about her?

"I'm pleased ta meet ya." Whoops. Tammy had

taught her to make her words clearer. She needed to remember all those lessons.

"Welcome to Crow Crossing." He reached for her satchel, and she released it to him. "Do you have a trunk?"

She pointed, hoping he wouldn't take note of the battered affair. She'd found it stored in the back of the barn behind the hotel and purchased it for a few pennies.

He told the porter to take it to the wagon that stood nearby. Then she followed him down the steps and accepted the hand he held out to assist her to the seat. Her breath catching momentarily, she quickly withdrew and interlocked her fingers in her lap, then allowed herself to look down at him.

He shoved his hat back so he could see her better. "Are you wanting to proceed with our plans?"

She wished she could tell if the caution in his eyes meant he was anxious to do so or having doubts. "I haven't changed my mind, if that's what yer askin'." She caught her breath and waited to see if he'd noticed the slip in her speech and released it slowly when it seemed he didn't appear to.

"Very well. We'll go to the church. The preacher is waiting."

He circled the wagon and took his seat beside her. His hands were strong and tanned. An outdoor man. A cowboy who rode horses and chased cows. His work on the ranch sounded exciting and romantic. The knowledge did nothing to relieve the fluttering butterflies residing in her stomach.

He flicked the reins and the wagon rolled away from the train station. "How was your trip?"

"T'was fine. Jest fine." Long, dusty, and many times uncomfortable. Not that she'd allowed more than a passing thought on such matters. No siree. Her mind had raced ahead to her destination and her upcoming wedding. She was officially a mail-order bride and very pleased about the fact. Marriage would provide her with the security she'd longed for most all of her life.

As they crossed the street, she glanced to her right. Several businesses. One sign read Luckham's Mercantile. The windows winked in the sun. The steps leading to the door were swept clean.

According to Luke's letters, they could get about everything needed because the town was on the rail line. Not that she cared. She couldn't wait to get to the ranch. And her new home. As a wife, she could finally count on forever. She resisted an urge to hug herself.

The church lay ahead. The building was all white with a bell tower. She glimpsed a graveyard behind it. Were his folks buried there? He'd lost both parents and some close friends—parents to a young child now being raised by his brother and his brother's wife. All things she'd learned from his letters.

They drew to a halt, and he helped her down.

Another spat of nerves shook her and she couldn't make her feet move.

"Shall we?" He crooked his elbow toward her.

Did he think she was hesitating? She rested her hand in the crook of his arm and took a step lest he mistake her hesitation for reluctance. Because she had none. She liked everything she'd learned about this cowboy—one of the Shannon brothers. He wanted a wife and someone to cook and clean. She was more than agreeable to providing it because she'd get something of far greater value to her—a forever home.

He held the door open, and she stepped into the cool interior of the church. A simple building with wooden pews and a wooden pulpit. Speckled sunlight drifted through the frosted glass of the windows. A man rose from the front pew and turned to greet them.

Luke guided her forward. "Miss Ward, allow me to introduce Pastor Ingram. He's agreed to marry us."

Honor greeted the man, her voice thready.

Perhaps he took it as uncertainty for he took her hand and squeezed it. "My dear, are you certain this is what you want to do? Because marriage is a big step, not to be entered into lightly."

Honor's voice returned to full strength. "Sir, I like what I've learned about Luke. So, unless you've got some reason to warn me otherwise, I am most certain."

Pastor Ingram released her hand and chuckled. "I

have nothing but praise for the young man. Indeed, for his whole family. These arrangements are not the ideal way to find a wife but if you both understand that what you are about to do is vow before God to remain faithful so long as you both shall live…"

"I am." Her answer rang with conviction straight from her heart.

"As am I."

Honor held Luke's strong words in the center of her heart. To remain there forever as assurance.

"Very well. Wait while I summon my wife and a neighbor to act as witnesses." The pastor slipped out the back door leaving Luke and Honor alone, facing the pulpit. A verse had been painted on the front of it. *Thou shalt love the Lord thy God with all thy heart, and with all thy soul, and with all thy mind. Matt. 22:37*

She couldn't tear her gaze from those words trying to decide if the way her blood thundered in her ears meant they were a warning or a blessing.

Or—she argued—perhaps she was simply nervous about the step she was about to take.

Before she could continue her mental argument, the preacher returned with a neat-looking woman at his side and behind them a buxom woman, fussing with her hair. Pastor Ingram introduced his wife and Mrs. Holt before he arranged them—Luke and Honor facing him and one woman on either side of them.

Honor concentrated on the words he spoke,

wanting to never forget them, nor the feeling of this moment as she sealed her future with Luke Shannon.

"I now pronounce you husband and wife. You may kiss your bride."

Shock ran down Honor's body and tingled her toes. A kiss? But of course, it was part of the ceremony, and now that they were married, surely a part of their life.

She turned toward Luke, lifting her face to him.

His eyes, now a silky brown, held hers for a moment then he dipped his head and brushed his lips to hers.

She closed her eyes and stood, unable to move, even when he drew back. Somehow, as if in a trance, she signed her name to the documents the preacher showed them.

Chuckling softly, Luke pulled her arm through his, guiding her down the aisle and out into the sunshine.

She blinked, drew in a long-overdue breath, and burst into joyful laughter.

"Shall we go home, Mrs. Shannon?"

Grinning from the depths of her heart, she allowed him to help her to the wagon seat, resisting an urge to lean down and kiss him just to see if it felt as good here as it did in the church.

Knowing he would be shocked if she did so, she sat primly facing forward but was unable to stop smiling.

The pastor and their witnesses waved them off, wishing them God's blessing.

Luke pressed his hand over hers. "I have a surprise for you."

"A surprise. How lovely." Though it was impossible for anything to better the joy of the moment.

A trickle of warning cooled her pleasure. How often had she thought things were going well only to have everything snatched from her? Not this time. Like the preacher had said, this time 'twas forever.

What would happen if he discovered that she'd gotten Tammy to write the letters she'd sent to him? He'd requested an educated woman for his mail-order bride and Honor could barely read and write. But she could cook and clean and tend children better than many schooled women. She'd give him a home he'd be proud of and where he'd feel welcomed.

It was enough to guarantee forever. Wasn't it?

* * *

HE'D DONE IT. He, Luke Shannon, had gotten married to an educated, refined young lady like his twin's wife. She wore a neat traveling outfit and her hair—as she'd told him in her letters—was blonde. Straw colored and coiled in a braid. But her freckles. Yes, she'd warned him she had freckles, but he imagined a sprinkling across her nose. Not all over her face. They were on her forehead, her chin, and even her eyelids. He'd never seen anything like it.

Her eyes had met his when he caught her as she

stumbled. They were a dark blue like the sky straight overhead on a warm spring morning. And somehow his heart echoed the feeling he had on such days. Full of promise and possibility.

Which made sense seeing as they were about to get married, embracing a future also full of promise and possibility.

Of course, he was a touch nervous. It wasn't every day he married a woman he'd only just met. Although many letters had been exchanged and he felt he knew her reasonably well.

She'd stood beside him, facing the preacher, and repeated her vows with enough conviction that he knew she meant them.

Then he'd sealed their union with a kiss. Even now the memory of it made him grin. And if he read her reaction correctly, she'd felt the same jolt of...

Whatever it was. He didn't know. But he sure hoped it promised more.

He turned off the trail.

She looked at him. "Is this the way to the ranch?"

"Not exactly. But it's part of the surprise."

"Very well." She sat back.

Did she trust him so easily? He would do his best to never give her reason not to.

The tracks of a wagon that had previously gone in this direction were barely discernable. The wheels jolted over a lump, and she bounced hard. "I'm sorry it's so rough." The times he'd been here before, he'd come on horseback, so he hadn't realized how uneven the ground was. Would she find it too much?

She giggled. Her eyes flashed. "'Tis an adventure."

"You're enjoying it?" He'd expected a city-raised woman to be wanting a finer ride.

"Lovin' it."

"Good. I recall how you said you couldn't imagine endless plains. You saw mostly a big wide river." They were about to crest the hill he aimed for. "Wait until you see this view." Minutes later, he pulled the wagon to a halt. Before them, lay gently rolling hills that descended into a broad green valley and then rose again up to the blue-gray granite mountains in the distance.

She stood and stared. She raised her hands upward. "I've not seen anythin' like it in all my born days."

Her comment seemed a bit...he wasn't sure how to describe it. Maybe she'd picked up some words and dialect from living near a major river.

He jumped down and offered her a hand so she could descend.

She drew in a deep breath and turned from studying the view. On the ground, she kept her face turned to the distant mountains, but she was missing the beauty nearby.

He touched her arm to get her attention. "Look at your feet."

Her gaze lingered a moment more then she looked down and laughed softly, the sound like bird song flitting over the grass. "Flowers everywhere." She knelt and brushed the pink blossoms as gently as... he blinked at the thought that came to mind...as gentle as their kiss had been.

She cupped her hands over a yellow blossom and then sat back on her heels and tipped her face up to him. "If this is the surprise, 'tis the best I ever had. Thank you."

His thoughts were racing madly as he studied his new wife...her freckled face and dark blue eyes. A phrase he'd mentioned to her in a letter came to mind. *God saw that it was very good.* Only he didn't mean Montana this time. "Remember that I said Pa saw Montana —"

"He said it was very good." Again, that gentle, bird-song-like laugh. "I have to agree."

"Come on. There's more." He held out a hand to pull her to her feet. She came easily, as light as a feathered creature.

"I don't 'spect it could get better'n this."

"It's a picnic. I thought we could celebrate our wedding this way." Suddenly his plans seemed lame. Shouldn't he have arranged for a special meal? Matt and Gwen had been welcomed with one at the ranch.

"'Tis a lovely idea."

Good so far. He took a quilt from the back of the wagon and handed it to her then brought out the lunch he'd prepared entirely on his own. The others knew he was planning to marry Honor, but he didn't want to share her with them just yet.

She found a flat grassy spot that allowed them to enjoy the scene, spread the quilt, and lowered herself to the ground, curling her legs under her and spreading her skirt to cover them.

He put the basket between them and sat facing her. "Our first meal together as a married couple. I'm sorry it isn't fancier."

Her smile lit her face and blended a bunch of her freckles into one. "Sounds to me like you're thinking somethin' man-made could be better'n what God has done." Her gaze circled the scene and returned to him.

Understanding her meaning, he grinned. "I certainly don't think that."

They studied each other. The Montana sunshine warmed his shoulders. Muted bird song carried on the scent of flowers filling his heart with an unfamiliar sense of... he didn't know what to call it. Joy. Anticipation. Expectation. Yes, that, and so much more.

"How does it feel?" he asked.

"To be here?" She waved an arm to indicate their surroundings.

"To be married." The words sounded hoarse to his ears.

She studied him so intently it was all he could do not to look away. Her gaze circled his face and stopped at his mouth. A slow smile curled her lips. "Feels fine. Jest fine, it does."

His chuckle was more pleasure than amusement. "Are you hungry?"

"I am, for sure."

"I'll say grace." He bowed his head, but words didn't come. His heart was so full. He cleared his throat. "Heavenly Father, You who made this beautiful world, who sends the sunshine and rain, who blesses the crops, You have now blessed us with marriage. Thank You for that. And thank You for the food we are about to eat." He paused. His words seemed so insufficient. "In Jesus' name, Amen."

" 'Twas a lovely prayer."

Did she seem hoarse or was it his own thoughts?

He drew the basket closer and folded back the towel he'd used to cover it. What would she think of the lunch he'd prepared? He pulled out hard boiled eggs and handed her two. Dill pickles wrapped in brown paper, hunks of cheese, biscuits he'd baked himself, a jug of cold sweet tea… simple things. Would she guess at their significance? A meal he'd planned and created entirely on his own, a celebration of their marriage. A gift to welcome her as his wife.

The beginning of a new life for both of them. One that brimmed with promise.

2

Honor looked at the eggs and biscuits in her hand. Had he done this on purpose? Or was she placing more importance on this meal than she should? But she recalled every word of every letter he'd written, memorizing them so she didn't have to struggle over reading the words. She'd asked him to tell her what sort of things he enjoyed. One of them was riding out on his own, eating a meal he'd prepared himself and enjoying the scenery, the peace and quiet.

She had asked him what he made for those lunches.

I like to keep it simple. So I boil some eggs. Take a handful of dill pickles. It seems we always have a crock of them. Cheese if it's on hand. And you might not believe this, but I've learned to make decent biscuits. Mind you, that is something I haven't confessed to my brothers. I'm not sure how they'd react. Either they would tease me, or they would demand I make some and share with them. I'm pretty sure it would be the latter.

It sounded perfect and she told him so. And he'd replied in the next letter that he'd take her for such a lunch if she thought she'd enjoy it. She'd said liked the idea. But she hadn't added the words that flooded her head. She couldn't imagine anything she'd enjoy more than a simple picnic with the man she'd married.

Feeling his patient waiting, she lifted her eyes to him. At the intensity of his look, her words baked to her tongue. She was caught in the heat of his gaze. She realized how long she stared at him. Her cheeks warmed and she forced herself to look at her hands.

Her answer came slowly from a throat that was strangely tight. "This is the sort of picnic lunch you told me you liked to prepare and take out on a ride by yerself." She returned her gaze to his. "I'm flattered to think you'd share it with me."

"You don't think it's too plain?"

"I think it's special. Thank you." No point in telling him that she considered herself lucky to get food as good as this. Especially after she'd lost her job. She hadn't told him why she was unable to get work, but no one wanted to hire a young lady who made their customers unhappy. Never mind the reason was because she didn't welcome the forwardness of the patrons.

"I know we've told each other a lot about ourselves but I want to know everything."

His remark jolted through her. She hated keeping a secret from the man she'd married but there were some things she couldn't tell him. "I'd like to know everythin' about you too." She heard her speech and realized she'd fallen back into carelessness in forming her words. Best be careful. She turned her attention to peeling the eggs he'd given her.

He was quiet for a spell as he did the same and then passed her a buttered, fluffy biscuit.

She sampled it. "Yum. Yer a good biscuit maker."

"Thanks. But that's about it for my cooking skills. I haven't had to work too hard at learning to cook. Up until recently, Merry did it."

Right. He'd told her about Merry and Roscoe, the young couple who had died a few months ago leaving the little girl that his twin and his twin's wife were now raising.

He continued. "Mind you, I can roast a rabbit over a fire and even bake biscuits on a stick."

"That sounds interesting."

"Pretty ordinary around here." He finished a biscuit and reached for another but simply held it. "You said you've worked since you were eleven years old. I don't understand why you would have to. Can you explain it to me?"

How could she tell him how it was without sounding like she wanted sympathy? Or even worse, without him wondering about her education. Surely, he would realize that a child forced to work had no time for attending classes. She'd learned the basics while Aunt Ann was alive, but her aunt had been ill, and Honor missed a great deal of school in order to care for her. Mrs. Johansen had been kind enough to give her further instruction when she helped the woman. That was the extent of her education.

Would he understand how desperately she wanted a permanent home? "My parents died when I was very young. I don't even remember them. My aunt—my mother's sister—took me in and gave me a home. Uncle was none too happy 'bout supportin' a child who 'twasn't his own."

"What happened when you were eleven?"

"My aunt passed on." Her breath caught. "Even after all this time, I miss my aunt." Even more, she missed having a home where she felt safe. She missed feeling welcome. "Uncle said he didn't intend to take care of me. A neighbor lady had three little ones and said she would feed me if I helped with them. Uncle allowed I could sleep in my old room. I'm most certain Missus Johansen gave him a little money to help with rent on the house."

"Was it a good place for you to be?"

"The Johansens?" At his nod, she continued. "'Twas fine. Their house was warm, and I got fed."

"What do you mean, their house was warm?" He leaned closer and when she lowered her eyes to avoid meeting his look, he caught her under the chin and tipped her face up, and waited.

Slowly, reluctantly, and yet longing for understanding, she met his gaze and was trapped, unable to look away from the demand in his eyes. "Uncle was often away and there wasn't wood to start a fire." The ache and fright of those days brought a sting of tears that she blinked back.

He caught her hands and squeezed them. "How cruel of him."

"I guess. I learned to find wood and keep it under my bed. Almost burned the place down trying to get a fire going. Mr. Johansen came to my rescue and taught me what to do."

"It sounds like they were good to you."

"They were."

"But?"

It surprised her to know he heard the hesitation in her tone. "They moved away. The bottom fell out of my world when I learned their plans."

He stroked his thumb across the back of her hand.

"But Mrs. Johansen had spoken to several ladies, and I worked a day at a time for each—minding children, cleaning house, running errands. I bought my own food and gave Uncle money for rent. I didn't see much of Uncle which suited me fine. He wasn't a kind person." She'd never admitted the fact to anyone. Not even herself.

"Did he beat you? Touch you?"

She knew what he was asking. "No. But there are other ways of being unkind."

"Like making a child work to support herself. Like withholding love."

A twist in her heart answered his question but rather than agree, she kept her gaze on his calming thumb.

"You said something about working in a hotel."

"Yes. But before that, I worked for the Abernathys for two years until they hired a tutor for their children." She caught her breath and waited to see if he would ask why she hadn't been asked to instruct them. When he didn't, she continued. "I told you about my friend Tammy. Mrs. Abernathy is her sister."

"From what you wrote I think Tammy was a good friend to you."

"The very best." Without her help, she would never have been able to send letters to Luke. She didn't intend he should ever find out the truth about who had penned them.

"Where did you go after the Abernathys?"

"That's when I got hired to clean the hotel."

"Something about your tone says it wasn't a good place."

He was far too clever. "Some men think a chambermaid should provide other services than cleaning rooms." She could not keep the disgust from her voice.

He sprang to his feet, paced away to look into the distance then returned and stood over her. "Did anyone… did they?"

She understood his reluctance to speak of what

might have happened and rose to face him. "I never let anyone get close enough to do anything but…"

His head came up at her but.

"A bit ago one of the guests got a little too friendly. I hit him a little too hard with the broom handle and broke his nose."

He stared at her a moment then burst out laughing. "Let me guess. That's why you lost your job."

At least he could see the humor in what she'd done. She let his reaction ease the pain she'd felt at her dismissal, the fear, when no one else would hire her.

They stood two feet apart studying each other.

Would he guess just how desperate she was for marriage? And if so, would he find her deception acceptable?

* * *

A WHIRLWIND of emotions raced through Luke. How could anyone expect a child to take care of herself? He thought of little Lindy. She was only four and thankfully Matt and Gwen were raising her. But to imagine her on her own in a few years… It was unthinkable.

Just as he was having trouble wrapping his mind around Honor's circumstances. Going home to a cold house, learning to take care of herself then facing unwanted attention from men at a hotel. His fists curled so tight his fingers hurt.

He breathed slowly to calm his anger. Then took

Honor's hands. "Honor—Mrs. Shannon—I promise you will never worry about your next meal, or if the house will be warm, or if people will want to take advantage of you. As my wife, you will be provided for and protected."

She swallowed audibly and blinked several times, but she couldn't hide the sheen of tears in her eyes.

"Luke, those promises mean more to me than our marriage vows." She turned her palms to his. "I promise I will take care of yer house, make ya good meals, and give ya a home full of warmth and welcome."

She was right. These oaths meant every bit as much as those spoken at church.

They both returned to the quilt and the rest of the picnic. Contentment settled over Luke. He'd done well to find Honor. She'd had to work to have a home and yet had found time for an education. She might even be a better choice than Gwen had been for Matt.

"I've been breaking a horse." Then realizing she wouldn't understand what he meant, he added, "I take a young colt and begin working with it. Teaching it to take a halter and follow me. After he's comfortable with my attention, I add a saddle blanket. The horse I'm working on now is past two and ready to be ridden."

She leaned forward, intent on what he said. "I saw pictures of a man on a horse. It bucked and twisted. Looked mighty dangerous to my way of thinkin'."

MAIL-ORDER BRIDE SURPRISE

He grinned at her concern perhaps mingled with distaste at how the animal was treated. "We don't break them like that. We gentle them. I believe it's important that they trust us and obey us out of that trust." Maybe not unlike people. Didn't trust make it easy to do things you might not understand?

Her breath released. "So none of that crazy lookin' stuff?"

"Not usually. Though—" He ducked his head so she couldn't see his face which just might reveal embarrassment and a touch of left-over pride. "Sometimes a young man gets it into his head that he can handle a wild horse."

She chuckled softly bringing his gaze to her. Her eyes sparkled like sunshine on running water.

"And might that young man be named Luke?"

He grinned. "It might be."

"Sounds like a story I'd like ta hear."

"You're sure? I wouldn't want it to lower your opinion of me." Not that he expected it would. He was merely teasing.

She tipped her head from one side to the other and gave him serious study. "Do ya think that's likely?"

He shrugged. "Guess we'll find out. Bear in mind I was only fifteen or so and maybe a little cocky."

She chuckled again. "A little, ya say?"

"Yup, only a little."

"I'll be takin' your word on that." Her grin lit her face in a way that he liked.

23

"As you should. Anyway, to continue the story—" though he didn't mind if they continued teasing— "I decided I could ride a green-broke horse." At her questioning look, he explained. "That means he really isn't broke but close. Pa had said he wasn't ready to be ridden in the open but of course, I thought I knew better. I put a saddle on it and got on. It bucked a couple of times but nothing serious. Then he got some silly notion and bolted. He cleared the gate and raced away."

Honor gasped and pressed a hand to her mouth. Her eyes were large blue pools and her freckles stood out like bright flares as she paled.

He didn't mean to alarm her, but it pleased him nevertheless to see she might be concerned for his safety. "I was out of control. I knew one of us would end up broken and bruised and maybe worse though I was as scared of Pa's anger as I was of getting busted up. We headed down a hill with a dry creek bed at the bottom. I knew the horse would surely break a leg there. I was doing my best to make the crazy animal turn."

Although it was a long time ago, he still felt those fears… of injuring a horse, of breaking every bone in his body, and the specter of incurring his pa's wrath. Perhaps he'd never be able to put them completely to rest. Which might be a good thing if it kept him from doing something so foolish again.

"Suddenly the horse turned and went one way. I went the other. Landed on my head and was knocked out. Riley and Matt found me and took me home. Not that I remember any of that part. Ma sat with me for three days as I went in and out of consciousness. It was knowing Ma was there and nothing else mattered to her but being with me that meant so much. I'll never forget that feeling." It almost canceled out his Pa's reaction.

"You said you were afeared of yer Pa. What did he do?"

"At first, he didn't say anything, and I thought he was going to overlook it. But he was only waiting until I recovered. Then he grabbed my shoulder and squeezed hard enough that it was all I could do not to squirm." He grinned at Honor. "He did that on purpose to let me know he meant business." He looked past Honor as he remembered Pa's words. "He said, 'Son, your reckless spirit might have cost you your life or that of a good horse. In the future, think before you act.'"

"That was it? Doesn't sound like much."

"You have to understand that I greatly admired my Pa and to know I had disappointed him was punishment enough. Not to mention the bump on my head." He rubbed at the spot that had long ago stopped hurting.

"Guess ya learned yer lesson and don't take risks anymore."

"I try and find my excitement in other ways."

She studied him a moment. "Such as your camping trips? Or ridin' into the mountains?"

"You could say that."

She chuckled. "Or maybe ordering a mail-order bride?"

He grinned, pleased that she saw it as an adventure. "It worked well for Matt. Should work equally well for me. After all, we're twins."

"But not the same, didn't ya say?"

"I did."

"So… it's all right that I'm different than Matt's wife?" Her eyes searched his seeking his opinion.

"Well, you're certainly different."

She touched her face. "The freckles?"

He nodded.

"I did warn ya."

"They kind of grow on a person."

She hooted with laughter. "They definitely grow on me."

There were other differences, of course. For one thing, Honor had a bit of an accent that made her shorten some words. That fact surprised him. He'd expected she would have the same refined way of speaking that Gwen did. But she wrote fine letters.

But such little things didn't matter in the long run.

"I'd love to ride a horse." Honor's voice drew his attention back to her.

"Have you never ridden?"

She appeared to be totally fascinated with removing bits of eggshell from the quilt when it could have easily been shaken off.

"Is there something you don't want to tell me?"

Her head jerked up. Her eyes widened. She blinked. "About ridin'?"

That was a strange question. "Yes. That's what we were talking about."

Her eyes returned to normal size, and she grinned. "I did try a couple of times. Once with Uncle's horse. He had made me mad about –"

He waited but she seemed disinclined to explain. "Why were you angry with him?"

She drew in a long, deep breath that lifted her shoulders. "I guess I was still expecting somethin' from him that he wasn't willin' to give. Like love and all that kind of stuff."

His heart ached for the way she'd been raised. Their dog got more kindness and affection.

Honor continued, "The Johansens had jest said they were movin'. They'd told Uncle. He looked at me and said, 'Don't think I'm going to take care of a kid who don't even belong to me.' Well, I didn't expect it, but did he have to be so mean about it? I stomped out of the house. His horse was standing there. I don't know what I was thinkin'. Maybe that he'd worry about me if I went missin'. Course I know now he never would. Anyways, I managed to get hold of the reins and climbed to the saddle, and kicked the animal hard. He moved faster'n I expected. It was all I could do to hang on. I figgered I'd be dead any minute."

"What happened?" he prodded when she fell silent.

"Mr. Johansen stopped the horse and put me on the ground. He said I should think carefully about my choices. Do things that would benefit me and not hurt me." She shrugged. "I've tried to follow his advice."

"Good to hear. That the only time you rode?"

"No." Her eyes flashed with humor. "There was a stable boy at the Abernathy's who was good enough to teach me a little."

"A beau? Should I be concerned?" He was only teasing because if the man had been a rival, she wouldn't have come west to get married.

"About Albert? Nope. He had his sights set on bigger and better things." She seemed about to say more, then changed her mind.

Why would she say that? As if she wasn't suitable? The young woman before him had managed to get a decent education despite the way she was forced to live. Her letters proved that and elevated her in Luke's eyes. And he meant to tell her so. "He could do a lot worse."

She met his gaze for a heartbeat then lowered her head to study her fingers. "I hope you always think that."

Her insecurity ached through him. Of course, she was uncertain after the way her uncle had treated her, but she needed to know things were different now.

"Not more than two hours ago I vowed before God for better, for worse, for richer, for poorer, in sickness and in health, to love and to cherish, until parted by death. I meant every word."

Her gaze jerked to his. "As I meant mine."

He heard the hesitation in her tone. As if she had to express her conviction but doubted his. He understood how her upbringing had been the cause of that.

But his faithfulness and care would soon erase all those fears.

Wouldn't it?

3

"We should continue our journey." Luke rose slowly as if reluctant to leave their picnic.

Honor shook crumbs from the quilt, folded it, and put it in the back of the wagon. She turned to take in the view again. "Never goin' to forget this."

He stood at her side. "We can come back as often as you like."

It was a generous offer but she kinda figgered that once they were at the ranch, there would be work for both of them to do. She meant to be the best housekeeper and cook he could imagine.

They returned to the wagon and Luke turned back to the trail. As they headed west, he pointed out landmarks. A big pine tree, a crook in the road because of a boulder, and far-off buildings of some neighbors.

"How long to the ranch?" She couldn't wait to see her new home.

"Almost there." They reached a branch in the road, and he guided the horses to the right. A few more turns of the wheels and he stopped. "You get your first glimpse from here."

Up the ridge, she made out a house and a barn. A cabin squatting to the left. She sat back, disappointed. Hadn't he said there were four houses—one for each of the brothers? Had he been untruthful? T'would serve her right for she'd been less than completely honest.

"You can see more when we top the rise."

So that wasn't all. Good to know.

They moved on. Passed the low cabin.

"That's where Wally lives." He tipped his head toward the structure.

"Your oldest hired man?"

Luke grinned at her. "You remembered?"

"I remember it all."

His eyes warmed as if her answer had pleased him. Good. She meant to please him in every way she could.

A big barn lay to the right as she expected. And a huge garden. He hadn't mentioned that.

They passed a good-sized house. A man stood in the open doorway watching and Luke waved.

"That's Andy."

"Your younger brother." Her gaze rested on the

other Shannon and the house built by his father. Andy had been given the bigger house because he was favored by their mother.

They continued down the trail to a house nestled in the trees. Somehow it looked lonely, and she caught her breath, hoping it wasn't where Luke lived. But they drove by.

"Riley's house."

"Your oldest brother." Strange that he'd said little about Riley. Only that he was a confirmed bachelor. Might be a story behind that.

Another house came into view. Looking cozy. Was this her new home? But the door opened, and a woman and child stepped out. Even without Luke's words, Honor knew who it was.

Luke announced, "Matt's house. There's Gwen. And Lindy."

The two waved.

Honor studied the woman. In his letter to Mrs. Strong who arranged mail-order brides, he had requested a woman like his brother had married. *Educated, refined, willing, and eager to live in the west.* Honor could claim the latter. She would prove to Luke that there were more important things than the other two.

But Gwen did look polished and efficient. Her hair tidy, her apron clean and in position. Even her wave was royal.

Honor was grateful when they moved on, and she

could no longer see the other woman.

"Your new home." She'd been expecting the house to be on the right like the others, but it lay on the left. They stopped at the far side of the house. Windows greeted her with a flash of reflected sunshine. Past the house, she saw the mountains in all their majesty. Imagine seeing them every day unless, of course, the clouds hid them from view. "It's perfect."

He chuckled. "You haven't seen it yet."

Compared to the rundown shack she'd lived in, it looked like a mansion, but she kept those words to herself. No point in giving him information that would cause him to question who and what she was.

He helped her from the wagon and led her to the door. "I believe I am supposed to carry you over the threshold."

"Why?"

He blinked. "I really don't know. Guess I'll make up my own reasons."

What a nice idea.

"It's to show how welcome you are and inform you that I am now your husband and will protect you and provide you with a home."

She hugged the words to her heart, knowing she would cherish them forever. "It's like a repeat of our vows on the picnic."

He swept her into his arms.

Giggling, she held to him for safety. She'd never

known a man's embrace. It was a delightful, exciting sensation.

He put her on her feet, his hand on her arm to steady her. "Welcome to your new home."

She took in a long breath to calm her racing heart before turning her attention to the place before her and gasped with delight. They stood in a homey room. There was a burgundy couch along one wall, and two soft-looking armchairs at kitty-corner to it. Some bookcases with a large selection of books. Her spirits sank at that. He was obviously a reader. Wouldn't he wonder that she didn't care to read? Her attention went to the window. She gasped and moved toward it.

A valley lay below them. The mountains rose above that. The house stood on a point of land allowing her to see down the valley in either direction.

"My father named it Shannon Valley." Luke had joined her at the window. "Pa insisted we should always be able to see God's great creation."

"What a scene. God has truly blessed me." She could barely squeeze the words past the tears clogging her throat.

"What do you mean?"

She tore her gaze from the window, comforting herself with knowing it would always be there for her to enjoy and she faced Luke. "I am blessed with you as my husband, with this house, and with a view of God's great creation. Like your pa said, it truly is very good."

His warm, tender smile told her that he appreciated her mentioning his father's words.

"I'm happy you're pleased but you haven't seen the rest of the house."

"Lead on." She wrapped her arm around his.

He led her to the first of three doorways off the living room and opened the door. "Bedroom."

She remained in the doorway with him. The room held a bed covered with a gray woolen blanket and a wardrobe.

He moved to the next door. "Bedroom."

Almost identical to the first.

They moved to the third room. It was bigger. The bed was wider with a crazy quilt draped over it. Each patch was edged by fancy embroidery stitching. A shirt hung over the wooden chair next to the wardrobe. A lamp and book waited on a writing table beside the bed. Obviously, his room.

"Ma made the quilt." His voice grew husky.

She squeezed his arm. "It's beautiful."

"Pa insisted we each build our own house. He ordered us to have three bedrooms in each. One for the parents and one each for the boys and girls."

Honor's insides froze. This was the room for the parents. For the husband and wife. For her and Luke. Their marriage bed. She'd prepared herself for this. Had told herself she'd not only be the best housekeeper and cook but also the best wife. But her heart beat so hard she feared he'd hear it and wonder what was wrong with her.

"You'll be wanting to see the rest of the house." He turned her away from the bedrooms. They crossed the living room and stepped into the kitchen.

Delight rose in her throat and released as a chuckle. "It's perfect." A heavy wooden table stood in one corner surrounded by four chairs. Plenty of cupboards. A large black and shiny-steel stove.

She looked out the window over the worktable. Every view was inspiring. Like living in a beautiful garden, watered by nearby rivers, and protected by mountains. "My work will be pure joy when I have this to look at."

"There's a pantry and storage area here." Luke indicated the doorway. "And a little entryway for dirty boots." He reached for the door.

But Honor wasn't interested in such ordinary matters. Not when the view beckoned, and her kitchen held everything she needed to prepare excellent meals. "I could start cookin' this very minute."

"I'm glad you're that eager to start work. But it's not necessary. I believe Gwen was making a welcome supper."

"Oh." She hadn't been able to keep the disappointment from her voice and immediately smiled hoping he'd not take offense.

"Everyone is anxious to greet you."

She'd gladly put off the meeting 'til she felt safer at being part of the family.

He must have read the uncertainty in her expression. "They're harmless you know. You might as well get the introductions over with."

She nodded agreement though it wouldn't be as easy as he seemed to think.

So many people to judge her. Would they realize she wasn't the educated woman she'd pretended to be? Would Luke's promise to honor his wedding vows apply if he learned the truth?

* * *

LUKE UNDERSTOOD Honor's anxiety over meeting his whole family. But he counted on them being on their best behavior.

She turned to study the room again. A smile curved her lips. She was obviously pleased with what she saw.

Shoot. He pressed a palm to his forehead. He meant to put a vase of flowers on the table, but it had slipped his mind.

"Honor, I'll bring in your trunk, then I have to take care of the wagon. We'll go to Matt's house about five." He glanced toward the clock on the wall over the table. That gave him a good hour. Time enough to make up for his lack.

He heaved her chest to his shoulder and carried it into the bedroom they'd share.

She watched, her eyes dark and troubled.

"What's wrong?"

"Nothin'."

Obviously, something was bothering her. But if she didn't tell him, he couldn't guess. He patted her shoulder as he passed. "I'll be back shortly. Make yourself at home. This is now your home."

She didn't move as he left the house.

He got into the wagon and headed for the barn, mentally reviewing everything. He'd stocked the pantry, so she had what she needed for preparing meals. It was all strange right now, but she'd soon get familiar with things. She'd learn to appreciate the others on the ranch. She and Gwen would have much in common and become good friends.

He pulled to a halt at the barn and jumped down.

Matt strode up to him and clapped him on the back. "How does it feel to be a married man?"

"Fine so far. She's everything I expected." Mostly. There were a few surprises—like her freckles but nothing to be concerned about.

"Good. We're all anxious to meet her. Especially Gwen. She'll enjoy having another woman here."

Luke grunted a response as he unhitched the horses.

Matt stood by watching. Wouldn't hurt the man to help but Matt preferred to watch Luke and complain he didn't do things right.

Luke laughed. Why was he being so grumpy? Only

one reason. His concern over why Honor appeared to be worried. He could put it down to meeting the others except she hadn't seemed that concerned at first. It wasn't until...

He groaned. Of course. It was when he'd taken her trunk to the bedroom. She was nervous about their first night together. He'd put her mind at ease when he returned to the house.

"Something bothering you, little brother?"

He shook his head. "You'll never let it be forgotten that you're twenty minutes older than me."

Matt leaned back and grinned. "Nope. Got to use every advantage I have."

Luke scowled at him. "Doesn't seem fair. 'Pears to me that all the advantages are on your side."

Matt slowly stood up straighter. "That so? Care to tell me what exactly they are?"

"Can't say as I do." He turned back to putting things away. Matt was the responsible one. Matt was the one people counted on. Matt was the one who won every woman they'd ever met. Which was all of two. But he wasn't going to win Honor. She was Luke's and Luke's alone. Which made him chuckle again.

Matt gave him a smack on the shoulder that went a touch past friendly. "You're always such a tease."

"Yup." He grinned.

Matt grinned back. "You do remember that I always know what you're thinking."

"Not always."

"Yup. Always. That's what comes of being twins."

Luke snorted. "We aren't the least bit alike."

"Maybe not but doesn't change that we can read each other's minds."

Luke refused to rise to Matt's teasing. "I've got things to do." He strode away but not in the direction of his house.

Matt followed on his heels. "Going the wrong way, you know."

"Aren't you supposed to know what I'm thinking? If you did, you'd know I'm going exactly where I want."

He reached the garden and stopped, hoping Matt would mosey on to something else. Of course, he knew Matt wouldn't. The man was as stubborn as the plague. And nosy to boot. He wouldn't leave Luke until he knew what he was doing.

Very well.

He opened the gate and went inside. He pulled out his pocketknife and began to cut the stems of blossoms.

Matt chuckled as Luke knew he would. "A bouquet for your bride."

"Seems appropriate." He continued cutting until he had a good handful of flowers then edged around his brother and headed down the trail to his house, Matt keeping stride.

"That's very romantic." Matt sighed in a way that informed Luke he was teasing.

"It's our wedding day. A bride should have flowers."

Matt patted Luke's back. This time gently. "Indeed, she should."

They drew abreast of Matt's house. "Luke, I wish you and your new bride every happiness. I'll see you at supper." He ducked into his home.

Luke shook his head as he continued onward to his own house. Brothers could be annoying especially when one was a twin, but they were also his best friends. He knew he could always count on them.

He stepped into the kitchen. Honor sat on a chair her hands clasped tightly in her lap. He stopped where he stood. What had happened to the joy she'd exhibited earlier?

What would it take to bring it back?

4

Honor couldn't pull a happy thought from her heart. She'd gone to the bedroom—their bedroom—as soon as Luke left. She took warm water with her and washed up. The suit she had on was dusty and dirty from the trip and she removed it. In the trunk, she considered her options. Oh, how she longed to put on a comfortable cotton dress such as she normally wore and exchange the fancy shoes for her usual footgear, but Tammy's voice echoed in her head warning her she must dress the part.

The gowns Tammy had sent were appropriate for social gatherings and going to Matt's house would surely be considered such. With a weary sigh, she pulled out the dark blue sateen one and put it on. The color suited her according to Tammy, but the material was hot, and Honor felt awkward in it.

She felt even more awkward and apprehensive in the bedroom and hurried to the kitchen. If only she could turn her hand to things that she was familiar with. Cooking or baking or cleaning. But Luke would soon be back. She plopped to a chair and twisted her hands in her lap.

The door opened and she jerked her head up. Luke was back.

He studied her a moment, his eyes dark. Was he seeing her clearly? Had he realized her failings?

"Honor, I brought you a bouquet." He held out a handful of flowers in every color of the rainbow.

She gasped with pleasure. She took them and buried her nose in the blossoms, inhaling the sweet delicate scent. "Thank ya."

"I'll get a container." He stepped into the pantry and returned with a Mason jar, filled it with water, and set it on the table.

He expected her to arrange the flowers, but she couldn't stop smelling them. The moment felt as fragile as the pink blossom beneath her nose. No one had ever given her flowers.

Luke squatted in front of her.

She lifted her eyes to his, saw warmth and...

Nothing more. She expected nothing more. Certainly not judgment... or disappointment... or anger.

If only she could persuade herself to believe that.

"Honor, I welcome you as my wife, but I am fine

with waiting to consummate our marriage until we are both comfortable. Until then, I will sleep in one of the other bedrooms."

Her cheeks burned, and she opened her mouth to protest. His offer went against her desire to be the best mate possible. But the words that came out didn't inform him of that desire. "Thank you. That's generous."

"We'll know when the time is right for both of us." He rose.

She was so grateful, she almost hugged him. Truth was, she wanted to be kissed again. To know if that pleasant excitement would trickle down her veins like it had at the church. Her cheeks still burning, she put the flowers in the container and fluffed them out. "So beautiful."

"They're from the garden."

An awkward silence followed his statement. Had they already run out of things to say to each other? She moved to the window. The view brought a peace that replaced her anxiety.

Luke joined her. "Ma often said that it was impossible to worry or fret when she looked at the mountains. She'd quote a verse, 'For the Lord is a great God, and a great King above all gods. In his hand are the deep places of the earth: the strength of the hills is His also.' I'm not sure but I think it's from the ninety-fifth Psalm."

Honor repeated the words in her mind.

"What are you thinking?" he asked.

She responded without considering how she would sound. "The God who made the hills and mountains loves me. That's comfortin'."

"It sure is."

To know he agreed and hadn't judged her speech, erased lingering fear and doubt. He was a good man, and they would find their way through these early days of marriage.

They lingered at the window, her shoulder against his arm. Not wanting to break the contact that she found strangely comfortin' she didn't move.

A large bird flew along the valley.

He pointed in case she hadn't noticed. "A bald eagle. See its white head. There's a pair of them in a tree down the slope and they're raising two eaglets."

"I've never seen one before. It's so graceful." She would have liked to tell him how pleasin' it was to see the uncluttered view. No mud. No noisy wagons and even noisier men. No people pressin' on every side. She let out a long, satisfied sigh.

He shifted to study her. "What was that about?"

"What?"

"That sigh."

She chuckled softly and then explained what she'd been thinking.

He leaned a little closer, putting more pressure on her arm, and bent his head. "I hope you won't get homesick and miss seeing people."

"Never."

"If you do, just let me know and I'll take you to town or to visit neighbors. There's the Dixons. They're a married couple with two children. And of course, you have Gwen within shouting distance."

She slowly, boldly turned to look him full in the face. "I believe I have all I want right here." She watched as understanding dawned for him.

His eyes grew that shiny golden color she'd noticed at the train station.

Was that only a few hours ago? It felt like a lifetime. And indeed, in many ways, it was. She'd left her old life behind and was starting a new one.

He dipped his forehead to hers. "It's sweet of you to say that." He lifted his head leaving her struggling for balance. Though her body didn't sway. The imbalance was in her thoughts.

"Keep in mind I won't be here all the time. I'll be out with the herd or doing other things. Then you might get lonely."

She'd miss him. She knew that already. But seeing other people wouldn't make her miss him less. "I'll be fine. Jest fine."

"I suppose you will. Seems to me you've been 'fine, just fine,' most of your life."

"I'm not sure what you mean." She eased back so she wasn't distracted by touching him.

"Your uncle wasn't welcoming. You took care of

yourself from the time you were eleven. You worked, went to school, and managed very well."

A lump the size of a cow lodged in her throat. He was wrong. So wrong. He'd assumed things she hadn't said, but had no doubt made it possible for him to think. She didn't dare correct him. "The Johansens were good to me and helped me a lot. So did the other families I worked for." Tammy especially had been helpful. He already knew that but not to what extent her friend had assisted her.

"How nice of them." His gentle smile eased away her tension.

"It was. I 'preciate what they did."

He looked at the clock. "We have a bit of time before we're expected at Matt and Gwen's. Would you like to see more of the place?"

"I would, yes."

He crooked his elbow toward her, and she wrapped her hand around it, resting her palm on his forearm, feeling his muscles.

The tiniest tremor of warning snaked across her neck. He was a strong man. Would he use that strength to her regret if he learned the truth about her? Tilting her chin upwards, she dismissed the notion.

They left out the back door giving her a chance to see the entryway.

"It's small." He sounded apologetic.

"Just right." She'd seen every size and shape and function of entryways. Usually back ones when she entered a house as a servant. But having had to clean in a variety of homes she'd also seen front entryways that were larger than the little house she shared with her uncle.

"What would you like to see first? The barn, the garden, the outbuildings…"

"Everything." She laughed. Joy mingled with pleasure when his laugh joined hers.

"This way. It's my private trail to the barn for when I don't want my brothers to see me."

"Oh? Got things to hide?"

His grin widened his mouth. "Sometimes a man wants a little privacy. Brothers think they need an explanation for everything I do. For instance, if I want to go for a ride alone, or take one of those picnics I mentioned, I go this way."

They ducked into a path beneath sheltering trees. It was so narrow she almost fell back but he pulled her closer to his side and she didn't protest. Instead, she buried pleasure in the depths of her heart to treasure.

The trail curved and widened, and she saw a row of small buildings.

"Storage sheds." Luke led her to the first one and opened the door to reveal a large number of tools—shovels, hammers, saws, axes. Everything a person could expect to ever use to do any sort of work.

"It's so neat."

He chuckled. "Blame that on Matt. He insists

everything is orderly. I wouldn't be surprised if he makes Gwen organize the pantry in alphabetical order."

Honor drew back, shock draining the warmth from her face. "Do you expect that?" How would she figure it out? Her heartbeat thundered in her head. She forced calming air into her lungs, grateful the pounding in her head ceased. Of course, she could figure it out. It wasn't as if she didn't know the alphabet.

He laughed and pulled her hand back to his arm. "I'm sure you can manage the house without my interference."

Relieved, she released her breath in a quiet sigh. "I believe I can."

They went to the next shed.

"Harness room."

"I can see that." Again, so neat and so many things from two saddles to strips of leather and bits of silvery things that she knew would be part of a harness.

The third shed was full of supplies.

She stared. "It's like having a store."

"I suppose so. But we have to feed the cowboys and provide rations for those at the line shacks." At her questioning look, he explained a line shack was where a cowboy spent the summer making sure the cows didn't venture too far away. "If they get up into the mountains, we'd never get them back."

They continued their journey, pausing at the cookhouse. She stared in awe at the room where a dozen men could sit around a long wooden table. The stove was enormous. The cupboards were full of dishes and cookware.

The bunkhouse was next— rows of bunk beds with a pot belly stove, table, and chairs in the center.

She swallowed hard. The place was far more inviting than the house she'd shared with her uncle.

They moved onto the barn, the musty smell was familiar and comforting.

Luke indicated the pasture to the side. "These are the colts we're working with." He whistled and the six horses pricked up their ears. Another whistle from Luke and one horse trotted toward him. "This is Sarge. I call him that because he likes to be in charge."

"He's beautiful." The animal was a reddish brown with a blaze of white on his forehead and four white stockings. "Will he let me pet him?" She raised a hesitant hand.

"Let him sniff you first." Luke turned to speak to the horse. "Sarge, this is my wife. You'll be seeing lots of her from now on and I expect you to make her welcome." Luke cupped Honor's hand in his and held the joined hands toward the animal.

Sarge blew moist, warm air over Honor's palm. Something so sweet she didn't have a name for it wove in and out of her heart, knitting together loose ends she hadn't known existed.

Even though she was reluctant to lift her hand from Luke's she did so and rubbed Sarge's neck.

He endured it a moment then turned tail and trotted away.

Luke draped an arm across Honor's shoulders. "He's surprised I have someone with me."

The horse stopped and faced them.

Luke laughed. "I wonder what he's thinking."

Honor didn't know what might be in a horse's head. It was difficult enough to sort out her own thoughts.

Did Luke putting his arm across her mean he was simply being friendly, or did he have tender feelings toward her? She guessed it to be the latter.

Would those tender feelings evaporate if he learned the truth about her?

* * *

LUKE KEPT his arm across Honor's shoulders as he steered her toward the garden. The power of his feelings toward her surprised him. She was his wife and, as such, he owed her his protection and affection. But he felt so much more. He didn't know how to describe it except to admit he liked the way she fit against his side as they walked. He liked her easy laugh and her honesty about her difficult life that she told without rancor.

They reached the garden, and he opened the gate to let her enter.

"Oh my!"

He chuckled. "It's big, isn't it? But we have to feed all of us—four Shannons, two wives, a child, Wally, and a dozen cowboys."

"But I don't see a weed anywhere."

"Both Wally and Gwen like working in the garden. I expect they'd appreciate your help if you care to."

"I'd love to. I had a tiny plot at our house. Uncle thought it was a waste of time, but he never complained when I cooked a meal for him using the vegetables I'd grown." She bent over to pluck a ripe pea pod, opened it, and chased the tender peas into her mouth. "Does someone preserve things?"

"Merry did before her passing. Wally does a bit, mostly for his own use. Gwen started filling jars as soon as she got here. You're more than welcome to put up what you think we'll need."

"That will be a wonderful adventure." She grew silent. "Who puts up for the others—your brothers and the cowboys?"

"I really don't know. Merry was the one..."

"I don't mind doing some."

"That's generous. You sure it won't be too much?" After all, she had to adjust to being his wife—though that should be simple enough—him being such an easy person to live with. He laughed at his private joke.

She lifted questioning eyes to him. "Did I say somethin' amusin'?"

He explained what he'd thought, pleased when she chuckled.

"I guess that remains to be seen, but so far, so good." Her gaze held his.

Something unfamiliar as desert sand sifted through his brain. He couldn't say what it was—awareness? Interest? Desire? He only knew he liked the feeling. He touched his fingers to her cheeks. Remembering the way his heart had expanded at their kiss—their first and only kiss—he leaned forward.

"Gwen's expecting us." Andy's call shattered the moment and Luke straightened.

"We'll be along right away." He waited until Andy went down the trail.

Honor studied the ground at her feet.

He dipped his forehead to her blonde hair and inhaled the clean, sweet scent of her. "Are you ready to meet the others?"

"Ready as I'll ever be." She stepped back and lifted her gaze to his. "Promise you'll stay with me."

"Always."

She chuckled. "That might be impossible."

He held her gaze with his own, his heart saying more than words could. "I'll be with you in spirit when I'm not present in body."

"Thank you." Her whisper barely reached his ears.

"Then let's do this." He took her hand and drew her

to his side as they walked toward Matt and Gwen's house.

The closer they got, the harder she squeezed his hand.

What could he do to make her relax?

5

Honor would give everything she owned to avoid this meeting. Except for the wedding ring Luke had slipped on her finger when they married. A simple gold band that she would cherish forever. Until death parted them as they'd vowed. He'd promised to protect her too.

But how was he to shield her from his brothers and from Gwen, all who might suspect the truth about her?

Till death part us.

She'd meant every word and assumed he had too and strengthened herself with that thought. But the closer they got to Matt's house, the tighter her insides twisted.

Gwen was from the same city as Honor. They might have crossed paths. Perhaps when Gwen visited one of the homes where Honor worked. Would she have noticed a servant girl? Or a nanny she'd only had a glimpse of?

Honor prayed not. She must be careful to watch how she formed her words.

Then another possibility caught her thoughts. Mrs. Strong had arranged both marriages. Would that connection be her downfall?

If only she dared tell Luke the truth. It bothered her a good deal to be living a falsehood. But she'd decided it was best to wait until he'd come to value what she had to offer before he learned her failings. Thinking of her dishonesty made her stumble.

Luke caught her. "Careful now." He'd assumed she'd tripped on the uneven ground. She allowed the mistake. Not that she wanted him to think she was always tripping.

They stood in front of the house.

She would have turned and run, just as Sarge did, except the door opened, and a man and woman called a greeting.

"Welcome to our home. I'm Matt. Luke's twin."

Matt was definitely different than his brother. Shorter, darker hair. A considering look as he tried not to stare.

"And I'm Gwen and so pleased to have another woman in my midst."

Oh my! If Luke expected her to be like Gwen, he was doomed for disappointment. Her brown hair was perfectly styled around her head in some sort of a coil.

MAIL-ORDER BRIDE SURPRISE

Her skin was flawless. She wore a housedress that made Honor's housedresses look like rags. Her voice was gentle. Refined.

Honor was never going to be able to speak that way. And heavens above, her face was a speckled mess.

Luke introduced Honor and she managed to squeak out a greeting before he edged them forward and into the house. A pretty little girl rocked back and forth on her feet as Honor entered. A smallish child with braided brown hair. And a wide grin.

"Hello. My name is Lindy and I live here."

The child's smile eased Honor's tension. She could relate to children. "Hello, Lindy. I've heard a little bit about you. I'm looking forward to learning more."

Luke drew Honor further into the living room.

Three men stood, waiting to be introduced. She would have recognized them even without Luke's words.

Andy, the youngest brother. Blond with blue eyes. He had a look of innocence.

Riley, the oldest. Hair darker than the others. Darker eyes that seemed to hold a dozen secrets. A man with secrets could well recognize that she had some, and she only met his gaze for two seconds.

And Wally. Older. Wiser. Kinder. Streaks of gray in his dark hair. And a gentle smile.

Introductions over, Honor glanced around the house. It was the same design as hers and Luke's. Only it was full of touches that indicated love and happiness. Little doilies. Polished lamps. A bookshelf full of books. These people really seemed to like reading. Was that how they spent the long winter evenings?

What would she do?

She noticed a sewing basket. She liked sewing and knitting. That's how she planned to spend her winter evenings.

There were pictures on the wall. One was familiar —a park in Kellom where she'd taken the Abernathy children.

She stole a glance at Gwen. Would they have seen each other there? She didn't recognize Gwen but that didn't mean…

Honor shrugged. No one noticed nannies and she'd been too occupied with her charges to notice fancy ladies out for a walk.

"Everyone come and sit. The meal is ready." The men stepped back and waited for Luke to guide Honor into the kitchen. Again, she was struck by how similar it was to Luke's house although the table was bigger. Welcoming aromas came from the food. The door and windows were open to chase away the heat of cooking. Even so, the room was warm. Honor wished she could loosen the collar on her dress. Instead, she sweltered in the heavy fabric.

Luke held a chair for her and then sat at her side. The others found places. She was at the corner and Gwen was at the end of the table so close she feared their fingers would brush if they reached for something at the same time. She squeezed her hands together in her lap and kept her attention on her plate.

"I'll ask the blessing." Matt's words jolted through her.

She had to stop being so nervous before it gave people reason to be suspicious.

Luke covered her fisted hands with his and her chest relaxed so she could take in a calming breath.

Matt's amen made Honor realize she'd been so consumed with her own thoughts and the comfort of Luke's touch that she hadn't heard a word of the prayer.

At the rate the food was passed around the table she concluded that the men must be starving. Worried she might choke, Honor took tiny portions. There was so much. Roast beef in rich brown gravy, a bowl of new little potatoes, lettuce—from the huge garden, she assumed. Green beans and peas. One taste and she knew they were fresh. She couldn't help but compliment Gwen.

"This is delicious. Thank you."

"You're welcome. I know you'll be anxious to take over your own kitchen and from what I understand, you are experienced—"

Honor wondered what Luke had said. That she was a working girl? Surely, they would wonder at her circumstances.

Gwen went on. "But if you need help at any time, you have only to ask."

"Thank you. I appreciate that."

"I guess it's too late to warn you about my brother." Matt's words drew Honor's attention. He shook his head and seemed sad or upset.

Luke groaned. "Matt, don't start."

"Start what? I only wanted her to realize we all understand that sometimes you are…" He shook his head and tilted his raised hand back and forth.

Wasn't that a sign for someone not quite right in the head? She narrowed her eyes. And from their corner, slid a glance toward Luke.

"Matt!" No mistaking the warning in Luke's voice.

What had she gotten herself into?

Matt continued with an injured tone. "Well, I think she should know that you like to skip out on work from time to time. What I'm saying is"—he addressed Honor— "don't be surprised if, on occasion, he decides to ride away."

She held Matt's gaze a moment, guessing he referred to Luke's admission that sometimes he liked to escape his brothers. She shifted her attention to Luke. "I am beginning to understand what you told me about a picnic."

She hadn't said anything that would give away his secret and yet it had informed him that she meant his private trail through the trees and his enjoyment of riding away to be on his own.

He grinned.

Honor ducked her head before the warmth in his eyes.

Matt hooted. "Don't tell me he has you mesmerized already?"

"Matt, dear." Gwen's soft words carried a warning and Matt waved a dismissive hand. "The truth is, I wish you both the same happiness Gwen and I have found." He looked at his wife with such open affection that Honor shifted her gaze away. It didn't seem right to watch them.

"Seems as I'm the oldest brother, I should say something here."

All eyes went to Riley.

"I'm not one for love and marriage. Wouldn't believe in it at all except for Ma and Pa. They'd made all of us hope for the same as they had. So, Honor and Luke, let me say that's my wish for you."

Honor couldn't think of what to say. Shouldn't Luke reply? She looked to him.

He blinked. "Riley, I think that's the longest speech I've heard from you in quite some time. Thank you for those words."

Riley cleared his throat. "Seems it needed to be said."

Honor found her voice. "Thank you."

Andy rumbled his lips. "Kind of leaves me out on a limb, don't it? I can't be the only Shannon not offering fancy words."

Honor couldn't tell if he was teasing or serious

until Luke groaned. "Sure hope you aren't going to deliver a speech."

"Of course not, though there are some things Honor, as your wife, should know. For instance, Luke's been known to be… well, a little too adventuresome. Right, boys?" He looked at the other brothers and they nodded.

Andy continued, "Like the time he came in from a ride with his trousers all torn and the horse as jittery as a fresh colt. When we asked what happened, he said he'd tried to rope a coyote and it hadn't gone well."

The others laughed.

"Or the time he decided to ride that horse Pa had told him not to."

"He told me that one." Honor's words silenced the men.

"Okay, boys. Now it's my turn." Wally leaned forward. "I don't know what Luke's told you, but I've been with this family even before they landed here twelve years ago. Fact is, I joined them on the trail and helped their pa drive the cattle to this place. I've watched these young whippersnappers grow up and take over the ranch after their pa died. They's all good men if you give them a chance. Only one thing I want to warn you about."

Honor's breath caught in her throat.

Wally continued, "That boy can eat like a starving black bear."

There were hoots and guffaws.

Gwen held up her hands to signal she wanted to speak. "First off, they all eat enormous amounts. But seeing as I married Luke's twin—"

"She got the better one, but you'll soon find that out for yourself." Matt looked mighty pleased with himself, and Luke groaned.

Gwen continued as if she hadn't been interrupted. "I just want to wish you as much happiness as I've found and if he ever gives you a problem, come to me. I might have a few tricks for dealing with one of the Shannon twins." She patted Honor's hand where she rested it beside her plate.

Realizing it was all in good fun, and that no one was offended, Honor sat back and enjoyed the teasing.

Lindy pushed her chair back and stood, crossed her arms across her chest in a militant stance that Honor had seen many times in the past with children she tended. "Don't I get to say something?"

Gwen and Matt grinned at each other then Gwen spoke. "Of course, you do. Go ahead."

She faced Honor. "I like Uncle Matt, but I like Uncle Luke too. Only difference is Uncle Matt is now my pa. So there." She started to sit. "Wait a minute." She left the table and rushed into one of the bedrooms.

In her brief absence, Gwen whispered, "It's the first time she's sounded as if she'd like to call you Pa."

Matt's eyes glistened. "I'd love it if she's ready. She'll be wanting to call you Ma too."

"Maybe."

Lindy returned with a beautiful doll. "Auntie Gwen made this for me. Like a real Mama would."

Gwen sniffled and Honor didn't look at her for fear of embarrassing her. Instead, she studied the doll. Made from fabric, its eyes and nose and mouth were so detailed it looked like a real baby. "It's beautiful."

"I know." Lindy returned to her chair and positioned the doll on her lap.

"Well." Gwen pushed from the table. "I do believe it's time for dessert." She began to gather up the plates.

Honor sprang to her feet and started to help. Then stopped. Perhaps Gwen wouldn't welcome it.

But Gwen's smile said otherwise. "Thank you."

Honor carried the serving bowls to the worktable where Gwen cut pieces of pie for everyone and topped it with mounds of whipped cream.

"I hope you like rhubarb." Gwen handed Honor two servings.

"Love it." She carried the portions to the table and set one before Luke and another for Wally.

"I noticed that." Matt's eyebrows quirked. "You served him first informing us he's number one in your mind."

"That's 'xactly what I meant." She expected her look held a touch more boldness and challenge than was appropriate.

Luke hooted and winked at her. Her face burned.

Her freckles would be as bright as flames. She ducked away hoping no one would notice.

"Good for you." Gwen set a plate before Matt and Riley then handed Honor two more plates and carried the rest herself.

Honor returned to her place and tasted the pie. "It's delicious."

"Thank you. You might find a few stalks of rhubarb if the heat hasn't turned them woody. I don't know what Luke told you about the garden, but you're welcome to help yourself to whatever you want."

Luke answered for her. "She offered to put up some of the produce for the ranch."

"That's wonderful." Gwen's gratitude warmed Honor's insides and she decided she would go at the first chance she got and see what she could find.

Lindy had slipped away from the table and now eased to Honor's side.

"This is my favorite story. Will you read it to me?" She handed the book to Honor.

Honor swallowed hard. She didn't dare look at the adults. Wouldn't they wonder at her hesitation? Were her freckles standing out sharply?

Was this how everyone was going to learn the truth about her?

* * *

LUKE COULD SEE that Lindy and the others would keep Honor here all evening, enjoying her company. But he had no desire to share her.

He pushed to his feet. "I hope you don't mind if I take Honor home. It's been a long day. I'm sure she's tired."

Riley ducked his head and seemed very interested in the empty dessert plate in front of him.

Andy grinned.

"You be sure you let her get right to bed, now." Matt almost choked on the words as a chuckle accompanied them.

Honor handed the book back to Lindy and rose. "I'll help with dishes first."

Gwen waved away her concern. "No. that's not necessary." She grinned widely. "I'm sure the men won't mind helping."

Luke held back a laugh knowing they'd sooner go to their own homes but wouldn't leave until the kitchen was clean. There was something about Gwen that made them all want to do what they could to please her.

"Then it's settled. We'll say goodnight." He took Honor's hand and rushed her from the room, ignoring the teasing laughter that followed them.

Honor let out a huge gust of air as they moved away from the house.

"How long have you been holding your breath?"

She shook her head. "I've been breathing. But guess I was a tad nervous."

"It wasn't that bad, was it?" He wanted her to feel accepted by his family.

She stopped, ran her hands along her arms. "I seem to have survived." Her grin informed him she was teasing.

He grabbed her hand again and hurried her across the path and up the steps to their house. As soon as he crossed the threshold, he realized he had no idea what to do next. Did he suggest she go to bed? But he didn't want to say goodnight yet. Could he prolong the evening by making tea? Or suggesting he would like some so she would make it? Or—

"Did you get a chance to explore the house while I was taking care of the wagon?"

"A little. Gwen and Matt's house is the same design as ours. Is that because you and Matt are twins?"

"It's because Pa designed the houses. Riley's is the same. Except—" He recalled the last time he was in Riley's house. "Riley is a true bachelor."

Her eyebrows rose in question.

"He doesn't care about how the house looks. If Wally or Gwen didn't feed him once in a while, he'd eat everything right from a can. Though I believe he fries eggs." He gave her a moment to consider that before he added, "In a cast iron pan he never washes or cleans."

Her eyes widened then narrowed. "I don't know if you're joshing me or not."

"Merry used to put on Roscoe's overalls and boots when she made an occasional trip to Riley's house to get the bedding to wash and clean it a bit. I gather from what Roscoe said, Riley doesn't care much for how his house looks."

She shuddered. Then brightened. "Sounds like he needs a wife."

"Riley prefers being a bachelor."

"Why?"

"Good question. I suppose it's because he expected to marry a few years back and the girl rejected him. Guess he's never gotten over it."

"Maybe it's time."

"That's up to him." But she had a point. It wouldn't hurt to plant a few suggestions in his ears.

A thought jerked through him. He knew exactly how to prolong the evening. "I have a gift for you." He hurried to the bedroom and pulled the package from a drawer, pausing long enough to look around. A blue dress hung on a nail. About the color of her eyes. Apart from that and the trunk at the end of the bed, there was no evidence of her having been there.

He returned to the kitchen. She should be sitting more comfortably to enjoy the gift and he took her hand and pulled her into the living room, guiding her to the sofa to sit. He drew one of the armchairs close so he could face her. He put the package in her lap.

She studied it then lifted her gaze to him. "I never got you anything."

"You came. That's gift enough."

Slowly, she turned her attention to the present, untied the strings, and folded back the paper to reveal the book he'd bought her. She didn't pick it up. Simply stared at it.

Was she disappointed? Had she expected something bigger?

"I remember you wrote that you had a book about the west you enjoyed and thought you might like this one too. It's about the Lewis and Clark expedition." Then in case she didn't know about them, he added, "They and their traveling companions explored and mapped this country in the early 1800s."

"That's interesting." She opened the book and quickly fanned the pages. "Thank you very much."

"You like it?"

She looked up at him. "Of course, I do." Her gaze slid away.

For some reason, her reaction troubled him. Then she covered her mouth and tried to hide a yawn. Tears sheened her eyes.

What was he thinking? She was tired. That explained her behavior.

"Are you wanting to go to bed?" It seemed obvious but he was reluctant to end the evening. Not that he could say what he hoped to gain by delaying.

"I admit I'm having trouble keeping my eyes open." She blinked as if to prove the fact.

"Then please feel free to go. We've got the rest of our lives to talk and learn about each other."

They both rose and stood inches apart, in awkward confusion. Did he kiss her good night? Or step out of her way?

They were husband and wife. Didn't that give him the right—even the duty—to kiss her? Ma and Pa had kissed often. And it had seemed right and proper even though he and his brothers had often groaned and pretended they didn't like it.

He recalled something Pa had said. *Begin as you intend to continue.* Sure, he'd been referring to instilling good habits with the colts but seemed it applied to other areas of life.

He leaned forward and brushed his lips gently to hers. Intending to be quick and …

He couldn't remember what else he'd meant it to be. Every rational thought fled at the touch of his lips to hers. Only great restraint stopped him from pulling her into his arms and kissing her like he'd never kissed a woman. Until now didn't even know how much he'd like to do that.

He pulled back, hoping she couldn't hear the thunder of his heart pounding like a runaway horse.

She kept her face down. Sucked in a long breath and released it in a gust. "Good night." The book clutched to her chest, she hurried to the bedroom, closing the door gently behind her.

He stared at the closed door. Had he offended her? Frightened her? That had not been his intent.

What was his intent?

He couldn't say.

He headed for the middle bedroom, choosing it for no other reason than it was closest to Honor. Should she need anything in the night, of course.

The bed seemed hard compared to his own. The covers were too short. Something rustled outside the window. Luke lay awake wondering how he could get Honor and himself over this initial strangeness.

Would it pass quickly, so they could become what Luke dreamed of?

6

Honor was so tired her bones ached, but sleep did not ease her troubled mind.

Books. So many books. How was she to hide her lack of education if the others were so interested in reading? Even Lindy. She could likely have read the child's book, but she'd struggle and stumble over unfamiliar words, and everyone would know.

With determination, she turned her thoughts to the good parts of the day. Luke had kissed her twice and both times her world had exploded with color and beauty. Why had no one ever told her—warned her—of the power of a kiss? She'd been kissed a couple of times—a quick little peck but had never imagined she could feel such an enjoyable jolt.

She smiled. Surely, he felt the same. It would be enough for him to overlook her failings.

Tomorrow she would cook for him, decorate the

house—though she had nothing she could use to do so. She'd convince him that she was exactly what he wanted and needed.

SHE JERKED AWAKE the next morning and looked around at the unfamiliar surroundings. Then remembering where she was, and her plans, she hurried from the bed. She chose the simple blue, cotton dress she'd hung up yesterday. She brushed and braided her hair and let the braid hang down her back. So much easier than trying to keep it secured to her head. With a sigh of relief, she pulled on her comfortable shoes and fastened them.

From Luke's letters, she knew he liked coffee and soon had a pot full on the stove. From what she'd heard at Gwen and Matt's last evening, she knew a hearty breakfast was called for. She mixed up biscuits and put a tray of them in the oven to bake.

Sounds came from the middle bedroom. A boot clattering on the floor. A muffled grunt.

He'd be out in minutes, and she quickly broke eggs into a hot frying pan.

He emerged, yawning and rubbing his hair.

She grinned at how tousled it was. "Mornin'."

He drew to a halt in the kitchen and a slow, easy smile filled his eyes and curved his mouth. "Good morning, my wife."

His words warmed her wary heart. "Coffee's ready."

"I'll be right back." He sauntered to the outhouse then returned and washed up.

She handed him a cup steaming with fresh coffee.

He took a sip. "Good coffee. What did you do different?"

If she explained that she'd given the grinder a good cleaning it would sound like she criticized him. So, she shrugged.

He took a larger mouthful and sighed.

It was nice to know that all the fuss about making good coffee at one of the houses where she'd worked was paying off.

The biscuits were done, and she pulled them from the oven. "I hope they're as good as yours."

He chuckled. "They'll be better because I didn't have to make them."

The warmth of his look made her skin tingle in a delightful way.

She put plates on the table. Gwen had used a crisp white linen cloth, but Honor didn't have a single tablecloth in her possession. She served up the biscuits and eggs along with a jar of jam she'd found in the well-stocked pantry that seemed to have everything a person could possibly dream of needing. Her breath eased out when all Luke said was thank you. No suggestion that she should set a better table.

"I'll ask the blessing." He reached for her hand.

As their fingers curled around each other's Honor relaxed.

"Heavenly Father, I thank You for Your many blessings. For food of course. But also for a wife and a home. I am grateful." His voice deepened. "Thank You. Amen."

Honor took his words to the center of her heart, to cherish. "No one has ever been grateful for me." She hadn't meant to say it out loud, but she was so amazed she couldn't keep quiet.

He still held her hand and squeezed it gently. "How'd it be if I try and make up for that lack by telling your every day how much I appreciate you?"

No words came as she blinked back a sting of tears and swallowed hard. She managed to nod.

"Good." He released her hand.

For a moment she felt off balance then sucked in air to steady herself.

He ate his eggs and six biscuits. "You're a good cook. I appreciate that. Just as I appreciate you." He must have understood her embarrassment for he chuckled and patted her hand. "You'll get used to it."

She doubted it but didn't say anything for fear he'd think she wanted him to stop.

He ate another biscuit and cleaned his plate. "Honor, my ma used to read from the Bible every day. I'd like to do that too if you don't mind."

Why was he asking if he could read the Bible? Did he think she'd object? Had she given him some reason to think so? She searched her thoughts but could nothing he might have misunderstood.

"I think if we read after breakfast, it would be a good way to start the day."

We? She hoped he didn't mean that literally.

"I have a Bible. It's in the room you slept in. Do you mind if I go there and get it?"

"Of course not." Her dresses were hung neatly, she'd made the bed, and her other belongings were stored in her trunk.

He returned with a black Bible, sat down again, and opened the pages. He read the first chapter of Genesis ending with, "'And God saw every thing that he had made, and, behold, it was very good.'" He closed the Bible. "God made us. I'm sure He says we're very good."

Her gaze fixed on the table in front of her. God saw her, but He wouldn't be saying she was even a little bit good. Not when she wasn't being honest with Luke.

Luke set the Bible on the nearby shelf. "Honor, I will be working around the place for a few days. Mostly I'll be with the horses. You take your time getting used to everything. If you have any questions, come and find me."

She nodded; her eyes still focused on the table.

"I'll be back for dinner around twelve. And we'll aim to eat supper at seven. That leaves you lots of time to explore or rest or whatever you want to do."

"I'll be fine." Except she was drowning in uncertainty and guilt.

"Then I'll be off." He paused at the door to grab his hat. "You'll do fine."

And he was gone. She'd do fine? At cooking and taking care of the house? Or as his wife? She wished she was brave enough to ask.

It didn't take long to find ingredients for stew in the pantry. Someone had kindly left her a selection of vegetables from the garden and a jar of canned meat.

She mixed up a cake and baked it. She looked at the bare walls of the house and wished she had pictures to hang. But she didn't. The only things she could add to the room were her mother's Bible and her book about the West. Which, if Luke took care to notice, was almost entirely pictures. She put them both on the bookcase along with the book Luke had given her. She pulled the latter out again and turned page after page. Words. Nothing but words. Then she discovered three pictures in the center, and she managed to read the words underneath. Lewis was easy. So was Clark. But how did she pronounce Meriwether or Lieutenant? She studied the next picture. More words she didn't understand. Sacagawea? She couldn't imagine what that was. Was that even an English word?

She snapped the book shut, put it on the shelf, and turned to face the room.

The walls of the house closed in on her. She checked the stew. It could simmer untended. She hurried outside. Not wanting anyone to see her, she followed Luke's secret trail.

In the cool of the shadows, her worries disappeared. She stopped, stared into the leafy sky and laughed. She was fretting for nothing. She could cook and clean and do everything Luke needed doing. Everything but read, and who needed that?

She sauntered along the trail, mesmerized by the shadows and the flashes of blue sky overhead, enjoying the bird song and in the distance, the sound of Lindy singing.

The trail opened up to the buildings. She swung by the storage sheds, and passed the cookhouse and bunkhouse. Seeing Luke holding a rope and guiding Sarge in a circle around him, she stopped to lean against the corner of the bunkhouse where she could watch without distracting him.

Man and horse seemed perfectly in tune with each other. Luke gave some little signal and Sarge obeyed. Round and round he went. Changed direction. Stopped. Started. Luke shortened the rope until the pair stood breathing the same air.

Luke took the rope from Sarge and stepped back. The horse trotted away.

Honor closed the distance to the fence. "I've never seen anything like it."

Luke coiled the rope. "How long were you watching?"

"Not long. Jest long enough to see how he trusted you."

"Nothing better than trust between a man and horse." He turned to watch Sarge. "Except maybe trust between a man and a woman."

Honor studied him out of the corner of her eyes.

Was he hinting at something?

But he didn't say anything more. He reached for her hand. "I'm hungry. Is dinner almost ready?" His fingers closed around hers making her feel safe.

"'Tis as ready as it's gonna get."

He led her back down the narrow trail.

She smiled to think he might have done it on purpose, so they had to crowd together.

He took two large helpings of the stew she'd made and ate the last of the morning's biscuits. He asked for seconds of the spice cake she'd made.

"It was a great meal. Thank you." His warm gaze caressed her. "I appreciate your cooking." He dipped his head closer. Might even have meant to touch his forehead to hers but the corner of the table stopped him. "I appreciate you."

She couldn't meet his gaze for fear if she did so and saw affection, her heart would burst with overwhelming emotion. She didn't deserve his sweet regard.

He pushed from the table. "I have harnesses to repair. I'll be in the harness shop if you are looking for me." He hesitated a moment before getting to his feet. He squeezed her shoulder as he passed her.

Only after the door closed behind him did she realize he'd said if she was looking for him. Not if she needed him. Was it an invitation? She jumped to her feet and rushed to the window to watch him going down the trail. She stayed there until he was out of sight then turned away and wandered from the kitchen to the living room as if hoping to find something to ease her troubled mind.

She ground to a halt in front of the bookcase and stared at her mother's Bible. Aunt Ann had read the Bible to Honor. What had happened to her aunt's Bible?

God above, who sees and knows all. I promise to tell him the truth. But I don't want to do it until I'm certain he won't send me back.

Back? There was no going back. Nothing to go back to.

She must be a good housewife. She returned to the kitchen and cleaned it, polishing the table and work area until they shone. What could she make for supper?

Someone knocked, sending alarm skittering up and down her. Sucking in a deep breath, she opened the door. "Wally, hi."

He held out a bucket toward her. "Brought some meat. I figger you cook this for supper and then you'll have leftovers for several meals."

She took the pail and thanked him.

"You findin' everythin' you need?"

"The pantry is full of supplies." What she needed couldn't be bought or grown or shared. Only telling the truth would provide her need.

"You'll do fine." He said goodbye and left.

She seasoned the meat and put it in the oven. She'd planned to let the fire die down and allow the house to cool off but now it wasn't going to be possible. Thankfully, a breeze came through the open windows.

Remembering her promise to write Tammy as soon as she arrived, Honor got paper, ink, and pen from her trunk and sat at the table to labor over the task.

Got here. Luke is nice. House—she made several attempts before she got the word correct. At least she hoped it was—*is nice. Lots of food. Like a store. I like the*—she couldn't figure out how to say view so scratched out three words and substituted—*It's pretty here. Honor.*

She folded the paper and slipped it into an envelope and glued it closed. Then labored over the address, printing it as neat as she could. Tammy had given her half a dozen stamps and she fixed one to the envelope and sat back, satisfied at having completed the task.

Now to hide the letter until she could take it to town.

She put it under her pillow and stepped back, pressing her hand to her chest.

Guilt and fear mingled in her. She closed her eyes, dread sucking at her insides.

What would Luke do when she told him? He'd made it clear that trust was important to him. Trust between a man and a woman.

* * *

LUKE'S THOUGHTS wandered freely as he worked the oil into a harness. Honor was everything he'd hoped for. Already his house felt like a warm, welcoming home. And his heart felt safe and blessed. Sure, they had a long way to go until they felt truly comfortable with each other.

What could he do to make that go faster? He made plans as he worked.

The door to the shed stood ajar allowing him to see past the bunkhouse and barn to the garden beyond the corrals. A flash of blue caught his attention, and he watched Honor open the gate to the garden and step inside. He observed her progress along the side to where the flowers were. She dipped out of sight. Moments later, she reappeared. He imagined her bending over the flowers as she had done on their trip from town.

Was it only yesterday? It seemed she'd been here much longer. Of course, she'd been in his heart since her first letter to him. An answer to prayer.

She ducked out of sight toward the middle of the garden and although he waited, she didn't rise again.

Guessing she was picking something, he turned back to his task, but several times returned to the door to watch and hope. Hope? What was he hoping for? A glimpse of her? That she might walk over to where he worked? Yes, to both.

The afternoon hours slipped away.

He saw her leave the garden, a basket in each hand, the baskets brimming with vegetables. She glanced his way. He waved. She smiled and nodded but went toward their house. He understood. She had work to do. Just as he did. But he didn't return to the harnesses until she disappeared from sight.

A few hours later, he finished and left the shed, choosing the path through the trees to get to his house. He stepped into a hot steamy kitchen. Rows of jars cooled on the worktable—red rhubarb, green peas, and orange baby carrots. The scent of dill informed him the carrots were pickled.

She brushed a strand of hair from her damp face.

"You've been working." It was on the tip of his tongue to say she didn't have to work so hard, nor do so much in one day but her proud smile made him hold back his words.

"Doesn't it look good?"

"Wonderful."

"Supper is right ready." She indicated the roast on the

corner of the worktable. By the time he washed his hands and combed his hair, she had slices of meat, a bowl of gravy, new little potatoes, and fresh peas on the table.

They sat and he reached for her hand. "My heart is full to see how hard you've worked and to sit down to this lovely meal." He shook his head. "I'm amazed and blessed." He'd thought Gwen was a good worker and efficient, but he doubted she could keep up with Honor. He again congratulated himself on getting a better mail-order bride than Matt had.

"I'll say grace." Words came from an overflowing heart. "Father God, thank You for Your many blessings. Thank You, especially for Honor. She's more than I expected. Oh, and thank You for the food." He closed with amen.

"Thank you," she whispered.

"For what?"

"For including me in your prayer." Her husky words scrapped along the inside of his heart.

He squeezed her hand. It would appear she'd had little appreciation in her life. Certainly not from her uncle. He would do his best to make up for that lack but at the moment, his stomach called, and they turned their attention to the meal.

They finished and he carried dishes to the wash basin then grabbed a towel to dry. She tried to take the tea towel from him.

"You've been working all day," she protested.

He hung on tightly. "The sooner it's done, the sooner we can escape the heat of this house."

"It sounds like you have plans." She tipped her head to one side, her eyes flooding with curiosity.

"Maybe."

Laughing, she plunged her hands into the hot water of the dishpan. "Then let's get this done."

She handed him a washed plate. He couldn't be certain, but it seemed she purposely let the water drip on his boot, and he chuckled.

"Are you trying to start a water fight?"

She batted big innocent eyes at him. "Why would I do that?"

He flicked his finger in her water, spraying it on her apron. "I don't know. Why would you?"

Her hands grew still.

Uh oh. What was she thinking? She lifted her wet fingers and flipped water at him.

He laughed. "Let's finish the dishes then take this outside."

The kitchen was clean in minutes, and he hung the tea towel and then reached for her hand. Outdoors, they ran down the path away from the house.

She tugged back. "Where are we going?"

"Do you want to see the valley?"

She shaded her eyes as she looked toward the west. "I can see it."

He pulled on her hand. "Come on. I'll take you to the bottom."

She trotted after him to the trail leading down.

"It's steep." He held her hand as they navigated the slope though she might have done better if she had both hands free to hold on to the bushes beside them but neither of them suggested it.

He paused before they reached the bottom to point out the nest of the bald eagles. The tree rose above the edge of the valley, giving the eagles a commanding view of their surroundings.

She stared up at the nest, suitably impressed. "It's a huge stack of twigs."

He grinned. "Gets bigger every year. Pa has a native friend who says it's unusual for them to nest this far south. He said it was a sign of blessing."

"Blessing for your Pa?"

"I think it's a blessing for all who live here."

"Me?"

"You needn't sound so surprised."

She studied him. "Guess I am."

He'd like to know why she thought it unexpected to be blessed. But then maybe if he'd been treated like her uncle treated her, he too might feel he didn't deserve good things.

He meant to convince her otherwise. He had the rest of their lives to do so.

They continued to the bottom and laughing for no other reason than the enjoyment of her company, he ran toward the creek, pulling her along.

They stopped at the gravelly edge. "The water level

has dropped. By fall it will be almost dry." He squatted and scooped a handful of water into his mouth. "So cool and fresh. Try it."

She knelt beside him and dipped her hands into the stream.

He waited until she slurped the water then cupped his hand and flung water at her. He was on his feet and backing away before she realized what happened.

She sat back on her heels and stared straight ahead.

He held his breath waiting. Had he offended her? Would she be angry with him? He took a step forward meaning to apologize and explain he only wanted to play.

She slowly turned to face him. Then before he could blink, she dipped her hands in the water and started toward him.

A second, two, passed before he realized her intent and then he jolted into action. But he was too slow. Or maybe he didn't try hard enough. She reached him and flicked water in his face. Cool drops that didn't matter any more than the breeze coming down the side of the valley. He caught her hands and pulled her close.

"Lady, do you think you can get away with that?"

Her eyes narrowed. "You started it. Or have ya fergot that?"

He liked the way her words broadened with her accent. "Forgot what?" He put his arms around her, anchoring her to his chest.

"'Twas payback."

He ran his gaze over her face. Such beautiful blue eyes. Like looking into the heights of heaven. And freckles that grew more attractive every time he looked at her.

She met his look openly. Freely. Honestly. Nothing between them. Not even air.

"I demand payment." He meant to be teasing but the huskiness in his voice likely revealed something different.

"What? Ya want money? Why I never heard such a thing in all my born days."

Before she could build up any more steam or pull away from his arms, he lowered his head. "This will do as payment." He captured her lips with his own.

At first, she was stiff and resistant then she melted against him.

The kiss lengthened. Time ceased. He was aware of nothing apart from the taste of her and the feel of her leaning into him.

She shifted and he pulled back. Stared down at her.

She looked up at him and giggled. "A lot of payment for a few drops of water, don'cha think?"

He grinned. "I don't know. Why don't you toss water my way again and we'll see?"

She freed herself from his grasp. "Maybe another time. Come on, I want to see more of this Shannon Valley."

"Very well." He let out a long sigh meant to inform

her he could think of other things he'd prefer to do but she grabbed his hand and pulled him along.

He went readily enough.

Being with her grew more pleasurable every hour.

They reached the dam. "It was formed when the bank caved in after a rain." He pointed to where the earth had given way. "Pa said it wouldn't take long before nature healed the scar, and he was right." Green grass and bushes left little of the formerly raw area.

They continued, her hand still in his, their linked arms swinging gently. She noticed little details like the tiny scarlet mallow flower that she claimed was the color of ripe tomatoes. And the seed heads on the maturing grass that danced in the breeze. They reached a good-sized rock, and he guided her to it, and they sat.

"It's so peaceful out here. Doesn't it make God seem closer?" Her voice was soft as if in awe of God's nearness.

Luke looked upward at the blue sky and puffy white clouds. "Reminds me of a Bible verse Ma often quoted. 'For as the heavens are higher than the earth, so are my ways higher than your ways, and my thoughts than your thoughts.'" He sat up straight. "I just remembered something. Seems like Ma always said that when things weren't going well. Like a reminder to herself and us that God knew what He was doing." His thoughts had gone back to times when Ma said the verse. "One time in particular —" He stopped. "Don't guess you're interested." He was only half serious, wanting her to express interest.

She jerked around to face him. "Tell me. I want to know everything about you."

"Very well. Then it's your turn. I want to know everything about you too."

Her gaze dropped. Her fingers curled into fists. He covered her hand with his. Of course, she would have unpleasant, even painful, memories. He wished he could erase those but surely, she had good ones as well and he'd like to share them.

7

Honor forced her lungs to pull in air and release it in a steady rhythm. She wanted to hear everything about Luke but how could she tell him stories about herself without revealing more than she wanted to?

Thankfully, Luke started talking, saving her from her guilty thoughts.

"One time we'd had heavy rains. It went on for days. Water ran through the yard. Pa and we had gone out to check on the herd. We ended up pulling five cows and three calves from the mud before we returned home. The rain didn't stop. Every day we had to go out and tend to the animals. It was a miserable few days." He shook his head as if recalling the time.

She imagined him wet, cold, and muddy and turned her hand to intertwine her fingers with his. If she was bolder, she might have leaned in and kissed him. Offering comfort that way.

He edged closer, almost sheltering her body with his.

"After three days of pounding rain, Pa was getting cranky. Ma reminded him of that verse. He growled that it wasn't God who had to pull cows out of the mud and ride in the pouring rain. Ma just smiled and said she'd trust God's ways."

"She was a good woman." Honor guessed his mother would never live a falsehood. And likely, Luke would not easily forgive one. Her only hope was he would understand why she'd done what she did. She'd tell him the truth... just not yet.

"You're right. She was a good person."

She thought he'd finished his story but then he continued.

"After the rain finally quit, we set out to check on things. That's when we found this dam had formed. Pa was surprised and pleased. It meant we'd have a good watering spot that lasted the summer." Luke gave a low laugh. "Pa said, 'I don't aim to tell your ma. She'd gloat that she was right.'"

"Did anyone tell her?" Seems the woman should have known her faith wasn't wasted.

"Someone did. Might have even been Pa. All she said was 'God's ways are higher than ours. We simply need to trust Him.'"

Oh, to have such faith. If she'd had a chance to

meet Luke's mother, perhaps she could have learned to be like her.

"Your turn." He shifted and gave her a demanding look.

Though maybe he didn't mean it to be so. Her own thoughts had made it seem that way.

"Very well." She would pretend she didn't understand what he wanted. "I'd like to see what's around that bend." She pointed down the valley hoping he'd forget his question.

"How's this? We'll go there once you tell me something about you that I don't already know. In other words, it can't be something that was in your letters." His grip on her hand was gentle, yet firm enough to inform her he wasn't going to let her escape.

"I believe I told you everything about me in my letters."

"Not a chance." His fingers tightened on hers. "There's lots I don't know about you. Where you went to school…"

Honor's heart forgot to beat. What could she say?

Luke continued, "Where you went to church." He gave a brisk nod as if making up his mind about something. "I know. Tell me how you came to be a Christian." When she still didn't respond, he added, "Or a time when you knew God had answered prayer."

She laughed softly as those words prompted a memory. "Mrs. Johansen talked frequently about God. Perhaps a little like your ma."

"Seems we both had a Godly woman in our lives." They smiled at each other, pleased at the idea that they shared something as simple as this.

Encouraged by the way his eyes took on that golden appearance she'd noted before, she continued, "I remember one time when all the Johansen children were sick, the littlest struggling to breathe. Mrs. Johansen did everything she knew to do. Sponged him for his fever. Gave him a birch bark tea. Put him in a steam tent. Both she and her husband were afraid they'd lose this little one. They talked freely before me even though I was young. Maybe twelve. I recall the Mrs. saying, 'Let us not forget that verse in Job, *Though he slay me, yet will I trust in him.*' Her husband said, 'Yes, they would trust God no matter what happened because God is love.' I guess that's when I first decided that if they could believe in His love that much, then I should too."

"I believe God had His hand on you to take you to a family that loved Him."

"They were good folks." Then before he could ask additional questions, she pulled him to his feet. "You promised to show me more."

"I did and I will." Hand in hand, they strode along the water's edge and around the corner. The valley widened and rolled away in gentle hills. The stream continued, a thread of blue in the otherwise green landscape.

MAIL-ORDER BRIDE SURPRISE

They drew to a halt as Honor stared. "'Tis a sight to behold."

"It's about to get better."

"I doubt that's possible."

"Come with me." He turned them back the way they'd come.

"What are you doing?" What secret did he have up his sleeve? Thinking of secrets... she darted a look at him. But she could detect no sign of anger or displeasure on his face. In fact, he turned and favored her with a flashing smile.

"You'll see. And I think you'll be pleased."

She couldn't hold his gaze though she tried very hard to do so. What if he saw the guilt and fear tugging at her heart and mind? Instead, she faked a little stumble—let him think she was clumsy—and turned her attention to watching where she walked.

He gripped her hand. "Be careful." He did not slow his steps.

They reached the dam and he stopped. Turned them toward the west. "Now watch." He pointed to the far side of the valley.

She didn't know what she was watching for but stood as he directed.

A moment later the lowering sun dipped between two mountain peaks. It turned golden, so bright she blinked. Orange, yellow, and pink brushed the water before them and colored the dips and rises of the valley floor. It lasted only a moment and then the color faded as the sun went lower.

Honor was full of amazement but empty of words. She swallowed twice and tried to find something to say. But still, nothing came.

Luke laughed softly. "Amazing, isn't it? I'm glad we didn't miss it."

Powerless to speak, she could only nod.

Luke pulled her forward. "The valley will soon be in shadows. I'd like to be up the trail before it gets too dark."

Either he didn't notice her lack of words or understood. They reached the path that would take them upwards before she could speak.

"Thank you for showing me that. I suppose you get used to seeing it but... oh my. It stole my voice."

"I haven't seen it all that often. You have to be in the right place at the right time."

"I'd say it's almost worth arranging to be there."

He started up the trail, holding her hand to assist her. "The sunsets are pretty spectacular at the top as well. You'll be able to see them from the west-facing windows."

The climb required her attention. She didn't speak again until they reached the crest where she immediately turned to see the western horizon. The sun was out of sight but had left behind traces of faded color.

Luke stood close, his arm across her shoulders. "What do you think of the country? Your new home."

"I am pleased as punch. 'Tis beautiful. The house is nice. Everything about my new home is very good."

"Very good, huh?" His teasing tone let her know he understood her choice of words referred to his pa saying God made Montana and said it was very good. Then he dipped his head to hers. "Everything?"

She realized what he was asking and leaned into him. "Yes, everything."

They stood that way for several minutes then he sighed. "Let's go home, Honor Shannon."

She could have pointed out that they were home, but she knew he meant their house. Hand in hand they returned. Inside, he pulled her close and kissed her gently then said, "Good night."

She reached for him, wanting him to stay with her, share her bed, hold her in his arms all night long but something held her back—namely the guilt that stained her thoughts. She must confess before they shared the marriage bed otherwise, he might think she'd tricked him.

Well, she had tricked him, but not that bad.

THE NEXT FEW DAYS, they fell into a routine, enjoying shared meals, and going for delightful walks in the evening, often down the valley but sometimes only going a few steps outside their back door.

During the day, Honor kept busy with cooking and baking. She went to the garden almost daily, choosing something to can. She tried to avoid Gwen, watching to see when the other woman returned to her house before she made her way to the garden, using Luke's secret trail so she wouldn't be seen.

Last night, there had been rain in the air, so she and Luke opted to stay indoors. He settled into an easy chair and opened a book.

She watched him.

He looked up. "Feel free to read something." He indicated the row of books.

"I might start a knitting project." She could make socks or mittens for him. If she had crochet thread, she might even start work on doilies. She liked how they looked in Gwen's house.

"It's fine with me if you relax."

Reading might be relaxing for him, but it wasn't for her. In her room, she pulled out her yarn. She needed more wool if she meant to make anything bigger than a baby-sized mitten. But she could start a scarf and add to it once she got more yarn.

As Mrs. Shannon, she assumed she'd be allowed to purchase items at the store.

Back in the living room, her needles clicked, and his pages rustled as he turned them.

It was a pleasant way to spend an evening indoors and when it was bedtime, he pulled her to her feet and brushed a kiss on her forehead.

She stared after him, feeling deprived. She wanted a real kiss. And his presence day and night.

. . .

THE NEXT MORNING, she bent over the row of wax beans, picking them and putting them in the roomy basket she'd brought. She tried to get enough produce to can a dozen jars and yet leave behind enough for others to pick.

"The garden is looking good, isn't it?"

Gwen's voice jerked Honor from her thoughts that had wandered down memory lane of the evenings she'd spent with Luke.

Honor slowly rose to her full height. "I can leave these for you."

"Nonsense. There's more than enough for us all." She started plucking beans from the vines. And she began talking.

"It's strange that I don't recall seeing you in Kellom. It's not that big a place. Or maybe I saw you but don't remember."

Honor gave a rueful laugh and touched a cheek. "You would remember a face like mine."

Gwen leaned back to study Honor a moment. "I suppose I would unless I only saw you from the back." She returned to picking and questioning. "I don't think I saw you in church."

"I don't recall seeing you either." Not that Gwen would have noticed Honor sitting in the back.

"Did your uncle work on the river?"

"My uncle was a jack of all trades. Sometimes he worked on the boats. Sometimes he delivered freight."

"My father and brother worked on the river. The Humbers?" She paused waiting for Honor to say if she knew the name.

She did not and shook her head.

Gwen continued, "Maurice Humber is my brother."

Honor understood Gwen was looking for a connection, perhaps thinking having one would give them something in common. But Honor knew otherwise. They had never been in the same social circles. About the only thing they shared was Mrs. Strong's mail-order bride arrangement.

"I don't recall any such mention." Not that Uncle talked about his work. All he ever said was 'Ya got money for yer rent?' He hadn't even told her he was leaving. Hadn't warned her the rent hadn't been paid and she would soon be without a home.

God had opened the door for her to get a beautiful home in the west. And a loving husband. She wanted the marriage to be real and honest. There was only one way for that to happen.

Today was Saturday. Tomorrow afternoon, after they'd returned from church, she would tell him the truth and beg for his understanding and forgiveness.

If she'd learned anything about him, it was he was generous and kind.

Would that be enough? Would it allow him to forgive her falsehood?

There was only one way to find out.

* * *

As Luke worked with the colts, he watched Honor go to the garden. She always used his little trail as if she wanted to avoid meeting any of the others. He wanted her to be friends with everyone, but especially Gwen. Given their shared past, it surprised him that they didn't have some previous connection. He put it down to Honor's unfortunate circumstances.

He observed Gwen also going to the garden. Maybe they'd find pleasure in working together. But a few minutes later Honor hurried toward their house. Her basket seemed full of yellow beans. No doubt she meant to preserve them today.

One thing he admired was her industriousness. Always working. She was a valuable asset to the ranch. Not that he cared. She was more than an asset to him. She was a friend and hopefully more. His affection for her grew with each passing day.

He grinned as he turned his attention back to the horses.

He was certain he saw fondness for him in her eyes. One of these days and soon, he expected she would invite him to share her bed. The thought of holding her throughout the night brought a broader smile to his mouth.

Riley had gone to town earlier to tend to some

business. Luke was in the pen with the young horses when Riley returned. His brother stopped at the fence.

"Your wife has a letter. You want to take it to her, or should I?"

"I'll take it." A good excuse to follow her to the house. He trotted over to take the mail.

He stared at the envelope. Mrs. Honor Shannon. It was the first time he'd seen her name. But what surprised him was he recognized the writing. It used to read Mr. Luke Shannon. But apart from her name instead of his, everything else was the same. Exactly the same. Even to the way the S was curled. He checked the return address. Miss T. Ross. Tammy? But—

He blinked to clear his vision, but the address didn't change. It was the address he'd sent all the letters he'd written to Honor. How odd. He shook the envelope and stared at it again. The writing remained the same. Had he really expected it to change?

Then he shrugged. Seems Honor and her friend had been taught penmanship by the same teacher. Though that didn't explain the same address. There had to be a simple explanation.

Dismissing his curiosity, he trotted toward the house.

The kitchen was hot and steamy. Honor glanced up from washing jars.

"Letter for you." He held it up.

She dried her hands and took it. Glanced at it and stuck it in her pocket. "Thank you. It's from Tammy."

He waited. "I noticed her return address is the same as the one I used to write to you."

"Yes." Then as if realizing he wanted a better explanation, she added, "It seemed safer to use her address."

Safer? From her uncle? That made sense. "You'll be wanting to write back to her."

She already had. "Perhaps I can take a letter to town tomorrow? Even though it's Sunday." Her voice trailed off.

"I'll introduce you to the Luckhams. They run the store and post office. They'll take care of it for you."

"Thank you." She turned back to washing the jars.

Feeling dismissed, he returned to his work.

SUNDAY DAWNED BRIGHT AND CLEAR. But Luke's head was not. There was something unsettling about seeing that familiar handwriting. He'd come to expect a letter from Honor when he saw it.

And even more unsettling was how Honor had hurried to her room after supper last night. She didn't even linger for a good night kiss. He'd hoped for more.

But today was Sunday. They didn't do any unnecessary work on the Lord's Day and he had plans for how he would spend it with Honor. The two of them on a picnic. If she was game to riding horseback, they could go up one of the trails.

He joined Honor in the kitchen for breakfast. She seemed strangely quiet. Then he realized this would be her first outing as Mrs. Shannon.

"Everyone is going to love you."

She jerked back at his words. Sucked in a gusty breath as if her lungs suddenly jerked into action. "I don't care if everyone loves me."

He waited thinking she had more to say, but she turned away to serve breakfast so he completed the thought on his own. *I only need a few people to love me and mostly, I need and want your love.*

A smile started in the depths of his heart and sped upward to his lips. Today seemed like a fine time to tell her he could offer her his love.

They ate breakfast and he took up the Bible. His mind focused on one subject—love—so he opened to the thirteenth chapter of First Corinthians. "Ma said when the Bible says charity, it's the same as love." He began to read, "'Charity suffereth long, and is kind; charity envieth not; charity vaunteth not itself, is not puffed up, Doth not behave itself unseemly, seeketh not her own, is not easily provoked, thinketh no evil; Rejoiceth not in iniquity, but rejoiceth in the truth; Beareth all things, believeth all things, hopeth all things, endureth all things.'" Slowly, reverently, hopefully, he closed the Bible. Expectantly he looked at Honor.

She sat with her head bowed. And although he waited, she did not look at him. Instead, she rose and gathered up the dishes. "What time do we leave for church?"

He looked at the clock. "In about an hour. I'll go see to transportation." Disappointment and uncertainty filling his thoughts, he left the house. He'd longed for her to lift her shining face to him. Her eyes gleaming with understanding of what he was trying to say. He would have kissed her if she had. Instead, she wouldn't even look at him. Had he pushed too hard? Hoped for too much too soon?

"Morning," Matt greeted him from the shed where the wagon and buggy were stored.

"Morning." Luke tried to put a little enthusiasm into his voice but of course, Matt picked up on the falseness of it.

"Things not going as you hoped?"

Luke grunted. He had no intention of sharing his concerns with his twin. His happily-married twin.

Matt continued, "Don't worry. Things will work out. Just give it time."

His brother was likely right, and Luke slowly smiled. "I have plans for this afternoon."

Matt roared with laughter.

Together they hitched the team to the buggy. "Pa was right when he ordered this four-seater." They grinned at each other.

"Our wives will enjoy the ride." Matt seemed pleased at the idea.

They drove to Matt's house, and he helped Gwen and Lindy to the front seat.

They proceeded to Luke's house, and he jumped down.

Honor waited inside, wearing the blue dress she'd worn when they went for their welcome dinner at Matt and Gwen's. She dabbed at her upper lip with a white hankie. She might be nervous. Or too hot. The kitchen was warm from breakfast, but she'd find it pleasant outside. He crooked his arm toward her, and she placed her hand in the bend of his elbow.

He almost regretted that the buggy was so close.

He helped her to the back seat and then took his place beside her. Gwen, Matt, and Lindy greeted Honor. Riley, Andy, and Wally joined them on horseback, and they were on their way.

She seemed to relax on the trip. But as soon as they reached town, he felt her tension return in the way she stiffened and tucked in her chin.

He covered her knotted hands with his. "I'm right here beside you. All the way." He lowered his voice. "Always."

She smiled though he noted it didn't reach her eyes.

He helped her from the buggy and led her across the dusty grass to the church.

Pastor Ingram and his wife greeted them at the door. "How are the newlyweds?" he asked.

Luke gave a smile that he guessed said far more

than any words. "We're doing great. Thanks." He guided Honor up the aisle, following Matt, Lindy, and Gwen to a seat.

A few minutes later, the pastor stood behind the wooden pulpit and greeted them.

They sang three hymns. Never before had Luke sung with more fervor. His heart was overflowing with gratitude for the woman at his side. He'd prayed before he'd asked her to come west and God had so wonderfully and generously answered his prayer.

Pastor Ingram opened the Bible before him. "I am reading from Romans chapter twelve."

Peace and contentment filled Luke as he listened to words that echoed in his heart. *Let love be without dissimulations. Be kindly affectioned one to another.* The preacher lifted his gaze. Those words would provide the motto for his home and his relationship with Honor.

"Dear brothers and sisters, we all know life isn't always easy. There are times it's extremely difficult. We suffer loss and despair. You all know what I'm talking about. How often do we let our pain dictate our actions? By so doing, we make the lives of others harder. We need to take to heart the words of the scriptures. Give love freely. Cling to good things. Treat others kindly. Rejoice in hope. Be patient in tribulation and never cease praying. Not only for your needs but for the needs of your friends and neighbors."

Luke nodded frequently throughout the sermon.

He had been greatly blessed and would do his best to bless others. And he meant to start with the woman at his side.

Today he would tell her he loved her.

The sermon ended and people rose. Neighbor turned to neighbor to greet them and catch up on the news.

"My letter," Honor whispered.

"There's the Luckhams heading out the door. I'll introduce you to them." He guided her down the aisle. They stopped to shake hands with Pastor Ingram and then stepped into the sunshine.

A fine sunny day. Perfect for the afternoon he had planned.

They reached the couple who owned the store and Luke introduced Honor. "The new Mrs. Shannon."

"Ahh." Mrs. Luckham's smile was wide. "The young lady who has written all those letters. Welcome."

Honor seemed to have lost her voice, so Luke spoke for her. "She has a letter for you to post if you don't mind."

"By all means."

Honor fumbled in the little bag she carried and pulled out a rumpled envelope. Her hands shook. Was she really that nervous about meeting the people of Crow Crossing?

He grinned. She'd soon enough feel right at home with these friendly people.

The letter fell from her trembling fingers and fluttered to the ground at his feet.

Honor gasped.

"I'll get it." Luke picked it up. And stared at the address. He recognized the address. It was the same one he'd put on his letters to Honor. But the printing was crude. The letters ill shaped.

Had she gotten Lindy to write the address for her? But why would she? Besides, he was almost certain Lindy hadn't been to visit. He handed the missive to Mrs. Luckham and guided Honor to the buggy.

There was only one answer that made sense. Only it didn't make sense at all.

But things fell into place that he couldn't refute.

She'd never said where she went to school.

The letter from Tammy held familiar penmanship.

Honor never read from the book he'd given her. Had looked unsettled when Lindy brought her book to Honor to see.

He'd been duped. She'd come under false pretenses. He didn't know who or what she was. But one thing was certain. She wasn't like Gwen. Yet again, Matt has gotten the woman Luke wished for.

He'd wait until they were in their own home before he demanded an explanation.

8

Honor fled to the bedroom as soon as her feet touched the ground. She was suffocating and she unbuttoned her dress, shed it, and chose a cooler cotton one.

Changing her clothing did nothing to ease the panic clawing at her throat that had started when Luke picked up her letter and had grown worse with every turning of the buggy wheels.

He would have seen her printing. What conclusion could he come to except that she wasn't educated? Wasn't who or what she claimed to be.

If only she could turn the clock back to yesterday. She would have told him the truth then. But there was no going back. Just as she couldn't hide in this room forever.

Luke was in the other room. She'd heard his footsteps cross the floor. Knew he was waiting, and she had no choice but to face him and face the truth.

The preacher's words this morning had both warned and encouraged her. Warned her to be honest but reminded her that evil could be overcome with good. Surely Luke would see that she had good. Enough good to outweigh what she'd done.

Lord of heaven and earth, please forgive my untruthfulness. Let Luke feel forgiving. Please let me convince him that I love him.

She sucked in air and stepped from the room.

Luke rose. His eyes were dark, unreadable. His mouth failed to smile a welcome. He crossed his arms over his chest.

A lump of clay landed in the pit of her stomach.

"Care to explain?" His cold tone sent a shiver across her shoulders.

"I planned to tell you everything this afternoon."

Not a word of encouragement. Not so much as a kindly look.

"Tammy wrote my letters for me."

He waited, as silent and unmoving as a rock.

"I can't read or write very much." Her words scraped up her throat.

"What about school?"

"I never attended. My aunt was never well, and Uncle made me stay home to take care of her." She could no longer look at his unwelcoming face and stared at the floor. "Mrs. Johansen taught me all I know. Which isn't much."

He made a sound that might have been understanding or disbelief or just plain disgust.

She waited for him to say something.

The minutes dragged on in deathly silence. Her lungs had seized up. She might never again get in a satisfying breath.

Finally, he shifted. "I'm a man of my word. I vowed for better or worse." He strode from the house.

Through the window, Honor glimpsed him going toward the barn. Would he come back for dinner or ride away and not return?

She dashed tears from her eyes. This was her fault. It was up to her to make it right. But she couldn't think how she would do so. Grief and fear robbed her limbs of strength and she crumpled to the floor and moaned. She'd endured loss and rejection before, but nothing that shredded her heart like this.

Finally, knowing there was no cure for her pain, no relief for her guilt, she rose. The only thing she could do was be the best wife, the best homemaker Luke could ever hope for, and pray that sooner or later he would see that was enough.

She stirred the stew she'd left simmering and set the table. And waited.

And waited.

He did not come and finally, she got up from the table without eating. She moved to the window, hoping for a glimpse of him. Lindy trotted down the trail, carrying a kitten. She saw a man leaning against the fence by the barn, but it wasn't Luke.

Where had he gone? When would he return?

She moved to look out the west window. The mountains shone in the bright sun but the sight of them did not ease the strain that made it hard to breathe. Memories of sharing sunsets with Luke ached through her like a fatal disease.

She dipped her head to the cool pane of glass.

The walls closed in on her and she ran from the house. Not wanting to meet anyone, she hurried down the trail away from the house. The valley beckoned and she made her careful way down the steep incline. Safely at the bottom, she clung to the side of the hill, hoping no one could see her. She hurried on, past the dam where Luke had shown her the flare of the sunset, passing the big rock where she and Luke had sat to talk. She continued until she went beyond the last place they had gone together. Only then did her steps slow and her breathing ease enough to relieve the pain in her ribs.

She walked for a time, doing her best to keep her mind blank... and failing.

Exhausted mentally and physically, she sank to a grassy area and stared at her surroundings. What if Luke sent her back to Kellom? What if he let her stay but never spoke to her again?

What if? What if?

Endless scenes and possibilities filled her thoughts.

Lord God, what I need is a miracle.

Words from the scripture the preacher had read earlier in the day came to her mind. She wasn't sure she had them exactly right, but didn't they say she should be patient in tribulation, faithful in prayer?

She would do that.

Thank you, Lord. I'll trust You to change Luke's heart so he'll give me a second chance. Or if he never does, please give me the strength to endure the pain.

Strengthened by her decision, she made her way back, struggled up the steep trail, and went into the house.

Luke sat at the table. His stare made her shiver. "Where've you been?" His voice deepened the shiver to her very bones.

"Out for a walk. Thinking and praying."

"Seems a little late for that."

Patient in tribulation, she reminded herself. "I don't believe it is. I'll have your supper on in a minute." She stirred the stew. It had grown thicker as it simmered but it would still make a tasty meal.

And she had a cake waiting for dessert.

She served the food and sat at the table.

He bowed his head but for the longest moment didn't speak. She knew it was hard to be thankful when he was angry. Finally, he mumbled, "Thanks for providing us with food. Amen."

Then without another word, he took a serving of the stew and ate it in silence.

Fearing he might again dash from the room she set a generous portion of cake at his side before he cleaned his plate.

He picked up the cake and pushed to his feet. "I'll be out. Don't wait up for me." And he was gone.

She tidied the kitchen and retired to the living room. She took up her knitting, but her hands remained idle.

Faithful in prayer. *Lord, please show me how to heal this injury I'm responsible for.*

Darkness fell and rather than light a lamp and sit waiting for Luke, she went to her bedroom, prepared for bed, and crawled under the covers. Sleep did not come until she heard him enter the house and go to the other bedroom. Even then, it was slow in claiming her.

He was gone when she slipped from her room the next morning. She made biscuits and coffee and fried potatoes. And waited. And waited.

Finally, his boots clattered on the steps, and he strode in.

"Johnnie just rode in from the line cabin in the west. Said he can't take the isolation any longer. I'm headed out there. Could you prepare enough food for a day?"

"When will you be back?"

"Probably be up there several weeks." He grabbed a handful of biscuits and left again.

He was leaving? How were they going to settle anything if he wasn't even there?

* * *

Luke stowed supplies in the panniers on the packhorse. He meant to be up in the mountains for a long time. Perhaps all summer. Maybe into the winter.

He'd speak to Matt about keeping an eye on Honor and making sure she had everything she needed.

He led the horse back to the barn where his mount stood ready.

Honor and Matt waited there, Matt holding the reins of a smaller horse. The sack Honor held was larger than what he expected for a lunch. Thoughts tangled in his head as he took in her cotton dress and boots. They grew more confused with the stubborn look on her face. Was she meaning to argue about his plan to ride out?

He looked from one to the other. "Good. I wanted to see you before I left," he addressed Matt. "I'll be gone for a while. See that Honor has what she needs."

"I've decided I'm going with you." Her words were firm. Even a little challenging.

Matt watched with avid interest. "Something going on here?"

"Nothing that concerns you." No way he was going to let Matt know that yet again, he'd been the lucky one. And rather than argue in front of his brother and cause speculation, he shrugged. "Very well. Let's be on our way." It was a full day's ride. And Honor wasn't used to riding.

Well, it was her choice to accompany him.

Leading the pack horse, he headed out, letting Honor follow.

They rode in silence for the better part of an hour at which time they traveled along the top of Shannon Valley to where the banks were less steep. He led the way down the gentle slope. For a time, they followed the stream. It was narrower and noisier here. He always stopped at a spot that allowed a particularly pleasant view of the mountains. Today, he glanced to the west but continued onward.

Honor stayed doggedly in his wake.

And just as doggedly, he ignored her.

And tried to ignore the constant nudging of his conscience. Was it only a few hours ago he'd sat in church, feeling so fortunate? Like the pastor said, they all experienced bad things. More of the preacher's words echoed in Luke's head. *We need to take to heart the words of the scriptures. Give love freely. Cling to good things. Treat others kindly. Rejoice in hope. Be patient in tribulation and never cease praying. Not only for your needs but for the needs of your friends and neighbors.* He didn't want to remember the words nor the way they'd made him feel.

They crossed the creek and continued, climbing now. The sun grew warmer and higher in the sky.

His stomach growled. Had Honor packed a lunch like he'd asked? Or had he ordered?

He didn't want to stop and share a picnic with her. It was a mockery of all he'd planned for this day. Instead, he grabbed the canteen of water and drank from it.

Had Honor brought water?

He would not turn and check on her. He didn't need to look behind to know that she was back there, still following.

His jaw hurt and he forced himself to relax.

His stomach growled again. Maybe he could stop long enough to grab something to eat. He pulled in beside a grove of trees and swung from his saddle.

"Did you bring food?"

"In here." She had two bags hanging from her saddle and she indicated one of them.

He unhooked it and looked inside.

"Cheese sandwiches." If she was tired, she wasn't revealing it in her tone or posture. "Biscuits with jam. Cake. Dill pickles." She looked at him, perhaps read his hardness for she shifted to stare straight ahead. "Didn't have time to boil eggs."

The memory of shared secrets and a shared picnic

on their wedding day tore through him, leaving nothing but bitterness and regret.

He grabbed food and handed her the sack.

She took a sandwich and a biscuit.

Seeing she had a canteen with her—likely thanks to Matt—the one who always got things right—he returned to his saddle and continued on his way... leaving Honor to follow or go back home.

Not that he had any hope she'd do the latter.

A woman who had left everything and come west to marry a man under false pretenses wouldn't give up at the first problem she encountered.

The sun clung to the top ridge of the mountains when the line shack came into view.

That's when reality hit him like a physical blow.

The shack was meant for a man alone. Not a man and woman. The only way he could avoid bumping into her would be if he wasn't there.

His stomach growled and it wasn't from hunger. How had he gotten himself into such a mess? More importantly, how was he going to get out of it?

How often had Pa told them that a man was only as good as his word.

He was dead certain that Pa had never had to live up to the sort of promise Luke had given.

Given in good faith believing Honor to be honest.

Honor! He snorted. She was wrongly named.

Just as he'd been wrongly treated.

They arrived at the shack, but he didn't dismount.

Lost in his dark thoughts, he simply stared at the building

His plan of escape had become a prison.

Why hadn't he changed his mind about riding out here as soon as he realized her intent? Now he was stuck.

Could he endure days of being near her?

9

Honor stared at the cabin in front of them. It looked small but adequate.

He dismounted and hitched his horse to the rail, but he didn't offer to help her down.

She'd never ridden so far or so long and had no idea she had muscles in her legs and back that could ache so badly. Biting back a groan she dropped to the ground. Her limbs threatened to fold under her, but she would not allow them to do so. She was here to prove to Luke that she was worthy of being his wife.

Unhooking the two bags from her saddle, she moved forward on shaking legs stopping when she reached the hitching rail to lean against it.

Still Luke did not look at her nor even in her direction.

His ignoring of her would have hurt more except

she was grateful he couldn't see the way she gritted her teeth.

Without a word he went to the cabin and pushed open the door. "This is it." He still didn't look at her.

Fine. She understood his anger, but she meant to stick to him through thick or thin, just as she'd vowed. And that meant following him wherever he went so far as it was possible, and she forced her shaking legs to carry her to the doorway where she stopped and took stock of what she had to deal with.

The cabin was rightly called a shack. The logs needed chinking. Daylight came through many places. Dusty cobwebs filled two corners. Imagining spiders racing across the floor and into the bed made her shudder.

Speaking of bed. There was only a narrow cot with soiled-looking blankets on it.

The furniture consisted of a rough wooden table, a bench, one hard-backed chair, the stove, and a set of cupboards. About as basic as one could get.

But nothing she couldn't deal with. Indeed, hadn't dealt with in her past.

She dropped her sacks to the table. "I'll have supper ready shortly." She'd planned ahead and brought the preparations with her.

"I'll take care of the horses." He slipped by without looking at her.

So be it. She'd played the tune and now she must pay the penny.

She explored the cupboards. Adequate dishes and pots. A few basic supplies. Some cans of beans and peaches. Two cans with no labels. No meat. No vegetables. It was a good thing she'd brought a few things with her. But before she would empty the sack containing her supplies, she would scrub the place. She'd need hot water, so she started a fire in the stove. It drew well. At least she had a decent way to cook and do other chores.

A pail in hand, she went outdoors in search of a pump. There was one close to the outbuilding. As she pumped water, she watched through the open barn door to where Luke brushed the horses.

He glanced her way. His gaze hit hers with enough force to make her arms stop pushing down the handle. And then he turned away.

Luke. The cry never left her lips.

He was angry. She understood that. But the pail of water felt heavier than normal as she made her way back to the cabin.

The water was soon hot, and she set to work, finding release and satisfaction in her efforts.

She put the meal to cook and then went for more water, intending to wash the bedding. Hopefully, it would dry before bedtime.

Luke poked his head out of the doorway next to the barn. "There are supplies in here."

She went to look, purposely stopping at his side, guessing he wouldn't be rude enough to move away.

Her thoughts proved correctly. It was all she could do not to lean into him as she took in the contents of the shed. "The walls are very thick."

"To keep out bears."

Bears? But she would not reveal the least sign of weakness. Something she'd learned long ago with her uncle. She pressed a hand to her chest, but it did nothing to ease the pain. Here she was in a situation far too like the way she'd lived with Uncle. She sucked in a long gust of air. The difference, she hoped, was that Luke was a kind and reasonable man.

"Looks like there's a good supply of basics."

"Beans, flour, cornmeal, oatmeal. The men out here don't usually bother with anything fancy. I'll bring in meat. In fact, I'll go get—"

"No need. I brought some from home and it's cooking right now. I'll wash the bedding. By then it will be cooked."

"Very well." He closed the door and walked away.

Very well, indeed. She hurried back to the cabin. She warmed the water only enough to take off the chill, scrubbed the blankets, and looked around for somewhere to hang things. No drying line. Fine. She spread the wet items over the nearby bushes making sure the wind was to her back so it would blow the things to the bushes instead of away.

She looked at the departing sun. What if things didn't dry before bedtime?

A shrug lifted her shoulders. She'd dealt with worse. But had Luke? Another shrug. He was a cowboy, who in his own words, liked to sleep outside. No fancy bed there. Besides, there was no way she'd sleep on that cot.

She planned to spend the night on the floor, curled up in her shawl.

There was one more thing she intended to do before she set the table and she dragged the mattress outside and proceeded to slap it with the broom.

"There. That should take care of dust and bugs."

She struggled to get the mattress back indoors and on the cot. Done, she rubbed her hands together. She'd made a difference that Luke couldn't help but notice.

Shadows lengthened across the path to the barn when she went to the door and called, "Supper." She waited until Luke came around the corner of the barn before she went back inside.

He washed at the well and then joined her indoors. He glanced around and she saw the spark of approval in his eyes.

She was prepared that he wouldn't comment but he said, "You've been hard at work."

It was enough and tension left her shoulders.

They sat across the corner from each other, he on the chair, she on the bench. She noticed his hesitation when she took her place but then he shrugged and said nothing. He bowed his head and murmured a quick grace—one she thought held less anger than the one he'd uttered at breakfast.

Her high hopes and great plans had been dashed to pieces in such a short time.

They had new potatoes and baby carrots from the garden and meat she'd brought from home. Home? Did she belong there, or would she be sent away? There was leftover cake as well.

It was a good meal, one to be proud of given the circumstances. He seemed to enjoy it and ate a good portion. As soon as he finished, he pushed back.

"I left the horses grazing behind the barn. I'll bring them in now."

"Of course."

He looked at the cot. "You can have the cot. I'll sleep elsewhere." And he was gone before she could ask what he meant. Wasn't he coming back to the cabin?

Patient in tribulation. Faithful in prayer. Yes, Lord.

As she cleaned the kitchen, she prayed for God to heal the hurt she'd inflicted upon Luke.

She checked the blankets. They were still damp. When the sun set, it got chilly this high up the mountains. But the cabin was warm from the stove. Almost too warm. She'd worked with the door open. The fact it also allowed her to watch Luke's movements was a bonus. He brought the horses in from the little pasture by the barn. He filled the water trough for them to drink from.

Watching him push the pump handle up and down filled her with so much pain she pressed her palms to her middle. Those arms had held her. Now they were shut to her.

He took the horses into the barn, and she continued with her chores.

Darkness filled the cabin and made it hard to see movement outdoors. She waited but Luke didn't appear. She lit the lamp and closed the door to keep out mosquitos and sat at the table to wait.

She yawned. She was falling asleep sitting there. Wrapping her shawl around her and rolling a towel to use as a pillow, she stretched out next to the bench where she was fairly certain he wouldn't trip on her if he came in after dark.

But to make it even safer, she left the lamp glowing, hoping he'd at least come to investigate why it still burned.

Tired as she was, she couldn't fall asleep.

Please, God, let him spend the night here.

Though she could not say what she hoped it would accomplish. Other than it pained her clear through to think she'd driven him to other choices.

* * *

LUKE STARED at the golden square of the window. Had she fallen asleep and left the lamp burning? What if it started a fire? He leaned against the corner of the shed watching and waiting for the light to go out.

Minutes ticked by. He shifted position to ease his legs. Still, the light glowed.

Exhaling his exasperation in a huff, he strode to the cabin and quietly entered, not wanting to awaken her. Not wanting to feel her wounded eyes on him. Though why she should act like she was the one hurt baffled him.

He stared at the bed. It was empty. His lungs caught in a painful spasm. Had she gone out into the dark and gotten turned around? He spotted clothing on the floor behind the table. He blinked. Not clothing. Honor.

"What are you doing down there? The bed is yours." He didn't mean to sound so harsh, but she'd given him a fright.

"I wouldn't think of it."

He exhaled loudly and shifted his attention to the empty bed. He didn't mind sleeping outside. Quite enjoyed it from time to time. But a bed with a mattress looked mighty inviting.

"The bedding didn't dry." Her soft words came from under the table. "Figgered it was warm enough to sleep in our clothes."

Warmth wasn't what concerned him. Her presence did. He'd been so close to revealing his growing feelings for her. Now he didn't even know who she was.

Certainly not honest. It hurt clear through to think he'd been hoodwinked.

But all he wanted was a good night's sleep. He blew out the lamp and stretched out on the bed. He was weary—not so much physically as emotionally. But he lay stiff, his arms crossed over his chest, as rest eluded him.

Finally, even knowing she probably slept, he asked the question that controlled every thought. "Why'd you do it?"

She shifted as if turning toward him. "I had a number of reasons."

"I would like to hear them." Not that anything would excuse what she'd done.

"For one thing I was desperate. I returned one day to find Uncle and all his things gone. He'd left without a word. For good, I assumed seeing as he'd taken everything but the stove." She spoke slowly, plainly, as if the discovery was an ordinary thing.

Not letting himself feel any compassion toward her for the way her uncle seemed to always treat her... as if she didn't deserve the least bit of consideration... he said nothing and waited for her to continue.

"I didn't have enough money to pay for another month's rent. I couldn't find a job anywhere. I guess you could say I was desperate."

Again, he waited, not giving her any encouragement.

"Tammy and I were walking by the church manse and Mrs. Strong was sitting on her verandah. She called us over and offered us a cup of tea. She held a letter and told us about the young cowboy who was seeking a wife. 'Educated and refined. A good cook and a good housekeeper' were his requirements. She told us what she knew about the cowboys of Shannon Valley. She looked at each of us as if asking if we were interested. We left soon after and Tammy said I should apply for the position. She knew I'd always dreamed of going west." Honor made a sound that could have been regret.

He had no way of knowing if it was so.

She continued, "I pointed out that I wasn't educated. 'Poof,' she said, 'you can cook and clean like no one else.' And she offered to write my letters for me. And here I am."

Did her last words hold remorse?

Well, she had only herself to blame for the change in their relationship.

She'd tricked him. Portrayed herself as something she wasn't and used her circumstances to excuse her behavior.

He stared into the darkness.

Would he have felt the same toward her if he'd known she was illiterate?

Flashes of the times they'd spent together burned through his mind. Memories of showing her his favorite places, telling her of his favorite things. That first picnic.

He chomped down hard on his teeth to keep back a groan.

They'd been so enjoyable at the time and yet now they were besmirched by her dishonesty.

To his disgust, he could feel her with every breath. He could hear every little shuffle and tiny sigh. His unwelcome awareness robbed him of much-needed sleep. Disgusted with himself, he rolled over toward the wall and closed his eyes.

HE WAKENED the next morning to the sound of the door opening and closing and bolted from bed. He knew what he would do. Exactly what he'd come here to do. He'd throw some food into a sack and ride out to check the far borders of the ranch and turn back any wandering cows. There was no need for him to see Honor for more than a few passing moments.

She returned with a bucket of water. "Morning, Luke. I'll have breakfast ready in minutes."

He'd like to say that wasn't possible but knew she was quick in her work. Already the coffee pot was full and on a hot burner. While he watched, she mixed up batter.

Pancakes coming up.

What was he doing standing here watching her? He strode from the cabin, washed up in the water trough, and took care of the animals.

By the time she called breakfast, he had his mount saddled and ready to go.

He parked at the table, feeling as cross as a starving bear. And not because he was hungry. It was all her fault for ruining things. He muttered a grace. Wouldn't have been surprised if God had sent a bolt of lightning through the roof at how his thanks warred with his anger.

But the coffee still tasted good. The pancakes were fluffy, and biscuits baked in the oven.

"I'll be leaving."

She jerked. "Leaving?" Her eyes were wide as saucers. And slightly accusing.

"For the day," he added.

Air left her in whoosh. "I'll have supper ready."

"No need to bother. I'll take whatever food you have ready and eat out there." He tipped his head toward the outdoors.

"Supper will be ready." Her firm words made him think she planned to stay up all night if that's how long it took him to return.

"Suit yourself." He pushed away from the table.

"Wait." Her sharp word stopped him.

She reached into the sack under the bench and pulled out something. She handed it to Luke.

"It was my mother's Bible. I've tried to read it but can only decipher a few words. You said you thought it a good practice to read from a Bible every morning. I'd be honored if you'd read from Mama's Bible."

He stared at the Good Book in his hands. He didn't need to open its pages to feel guilt staining his insides. Nor did he need to remember the preacher's words from yesterday. He was familiar with verses about forgiveness.

But he couldn't bring himself to forgive her.

He could not let her guess at his struggle. He let the pages fall open where they would and stared at the verses before him. *Therefore to him that knoweth to do good, and doeth it not, to him it is sin.* He blinked. That couldn't mean him. Except he knew it did. He flipped a few pages looking for something less condemning. *Knowing this, that the trying of your faith worketh patience.* Well, maybe he didn't want any more patience. He flipped pages again, determined to read whatever he saw.

He cleared his throat. "Luke chapter four, verse eighteen, 'The Spirt of the Lord is upon me...'" Every word a spear to his conscience, he read the rest of the verse without letting any of the words mean anything.

He closed the Bible, set it on the table, and pushed to his feet. "If you'd be so kind as to put some food in a sack for me, I'll head out to check on the cows." He strode from the room without a backward look. Without an inward look. He went to get his horse and rode to the house. He reached out for the food Honor held out to him.

She called, "Goodbye."

He didn't so much as lift a hand to wave.

This was all her fault. She'd ruined everything. Even the mountains failed to change his mood.

He rode all day. Turned back a dozen cows that had followed green grass and a tumbling stream out of bounds. He stopped at noon by that water and enjoyed his lunch.

He rode higher. Not that he expected to find any animals up there but if he went far enough, he might outride his anger. His pain. His disappointment.

But the afternoon sun was behind the mountain tops, and he still carried his troubled load.

With a grunt of disgust, he turned back.

Though he could not explain what he hoped he'd gain by going back to the cabin. Besides a hot meal and a soft bed.

His horse was in a hurry to get back to the barn and galloped along the grassy slope, slowing only to navigate through rocky portions.

The horse snorted and shied to one side.

Luke was instantly alert. He slipped his rifle from its boot and looked around to see what had spooked his mount. Not seeing anything, he eased forward, the horse still edgy.

They'd taken a few steps when he saw what it was. A bear hoofing into the underbrush a distance away.

They were close enough to the cabin that the bear would have smelled the food cooking.

A free meal would call to the animal.

He might be disappointed in her, but he didn't want anything bad to happen to her.

He fired a shot at the animal knowing he was too far to hit him but wanting to warn it to stay away. The bear hurried up the hillside and out of sight. Hopefully realizing it wasn't a safe place for him.

Luke stowed his rifle, bent low, and urged his horse to a gallop.

10

At the sound of a horse approaching, coming fast, Honor pressed her hand to her throat. Her rapid pulse beat against her fingertips.

Luke was returning. At a gallop. Was he anxious to get back to her?

Or was there some other reason? She looked around. Saw nothing to concern her.

Had he been hurt?

She stood at the door waiting.

He came into sight. Skidded to a halt at the cabin. Looked at her with dark eyes that revealed nothing then turned the horse and went toward the barn.

The table had been set for a time. She'd prepared food that would stay edible no matter how late he was. A thick soup waited on the stove—full of meat and vegetables—a nourishing meal in itself. Another batch of biscuits was in a bowl, covered with a clean towel.

She'd baked beans too. They would improve with slow roasting overnight, but they were cooked enough he could eat some now if he wanted.

Wouldn't he be surprised at the dessert she'd made?

She set the pot of soup in the center of the table and place the biscuits beside it. She stood by the stove waiting, knowing it would take a bit of time to take care of his horse.

Finally, she heard the thud of his boots and her lungs forgot to work.

He stepped inside and took a look around, glancing at her but not meeting her eyes.

Faithful in prayer. She'd prayed throughout the day for healing between them but knew it would take time. *Patient in tribulation.*

She indicated the meal, and he sat on the chair as she took a place on the bench.

For a second, he stared at his bowl, and she wondered if he would neglect to say grace. His shoulders rose and fell, and he bowed his head. "God, thanks for taking care of us and providing food. Amen."

Was there a reason he'd specifically added, 'taking care of us' to his previous grace?

"How was your day?" Would he tell her if something had happened to him out there?

He shrugged. "Turned back some cows. Rode lots." He concentrated on the bowl before him.

"I remember how you wrote that you enjoyed

riding in the mountains." Her spoon was poised halfway to her mouth. Would he object to her mentioning the letters that had gone between them?

"Yeah." His attention remained on his food.

Fearing he might leave the table without finishing, she served him a generous wedge of the pie she'd baked.

He eyed it a moment and tasted it. "Where did you find the berries?"

"Up the hill behind the cabin."

His hands rested beside his plate.

She stiffened. Had she said or done something not right? Besides let Tammy write letters for her, of course? But it seemed something else had annoyed him.

She wasn't one for beating around the bush. "Is something wrong?"

"Stay away from the berries."

"Huh?" Why would she ignore an abundance of free, fresh food?

"Do as I say."

"Do you mind telling me why?"

His head came up. His eyes were cold and hard. "Do I need to?"

She lowered his gaze. "Of course not." Her piece of pie sat untouched in front of her. And remained untouched as he finished his.

He pushed from the table. "I'll check on the horses."

And he was gone. Along with her hope and expectations. *Lord, I'm not finding it easy to be patient.* Dusk filled the cabin, echoing the darkness in her heart. She lit a lamp. It brightened the inside of the place but did nothing to ease the dark hollow inside her chest.

She quickly cleaned up and wrapped herself in her shawl and again lay down out of the way by the table. Luke would be tired when he came in. If he came in. A clean bed waited for him.

His footsteps thudded outside the door. He stepped into the cabin, turned out the lamp, and settled on the bed. His boots hit the floor. The bed squeaked as he got comfortable. Then heavy silence filled the room.

She tried to relax. Told herself things would get better. She only needed to be patient and trust God.

"I saw a bear." Luke's words startled her. "Not too far from here. Bears like berries."

She smiled. He was only concerned for her safety in case a bear came across her while she was picking berries.

"Thanks." Her one word carried a load of gratitude.

He gave a sound of acknowledgment. That was all. But it was enough.

For now.

THE NEXT MORNING, she scooted out from under the table. He sat on the edge of his bed, pulling on his boots.

"Good morning." She hoped he'd respond to her cheerful greeting.

"Guess that remains to be seen."

Well, it might not be cheerful, but it was something.

He strode from the little dwelling and headed for the barn.

Breakfast was ready when he returned, leading his horse. He tied the animal to the hitching rail. She served Johnny cake with the baked beans. The few eggs she'd packed carefully to bring wouldn't last much longer but they made for good baking while they did.

Luke ate heartily. He finished and pushed his chair back.

Before he could leave, she handed him her mother's Bible.

His mouth twitched as if he'd felt pain and then he opened and flipped the pages and read. "'The steadfast love of the Lord never ceases; his mercies never come to an end; they are new every morning, great is your faithfulness.'"

She was almost certain he gave no thought to his choice of verses, but the words were the comfort and encouragement she needed.

"I'd like food for the day. Please." The latter word was added as an afterthought, but it was a start.

"I've prepared it for you." Some Johnny cake, some pie, and a tin bowl with a screw-top lid full of beans.

Plenty of each. He wouldn't go hungry. "Supper will be ready when you get back."

He took the sack. "Thanks." He seemed about to say something more than stopped himself.

She followed him outside to bid him goodbye. "Watch out for bears."

He swung into the saddle. "You too." And then he was off.

She watched until he was out of sight and then with a slow, impatient sigh, turned back inside. It didn't take long to clean up from breakfast. She didn't need to do any cooking for several hours.

The day stretched out, impossibly quiet and lonely.

She wouldn't go up the hill to the berry patch though it was tempting. But was it safe to follow the trail downhill? The trees didn't crowd to the side, allowing her to see anything that might be hiding there in plenty of time for her to retreat.

Deciding she would keep a sharp eye out for any bears or other wildlife that might be dangerous, and she wouldn't go far, she wandered down the path.

OVER THE FOLLOWING DAYS, life went along much the same. She cooked and cleaned. She scrubbed the shelves in the storage shed. She explored the barn. She walked up and down the trail and circled the outbuilding. And generally tried to keep herself amused. She hadn't brought writing material, or she might have scratched off a letter to Tammy.

She tried reading the Bible but far too many words were impossible for her. She looked for the verses he'd read, hoping to find them, and knowing the words, be able to read them herself.

Finally, on the third day, she found one. *The steadfast love of the Lord never ceases; his mercies never come to an end; they are new every morning, great is your faithfulness.*

She read the words over and over, committing them to memory so she wouldn't need to find them and read them.

God, thank you for this encouragement. I trust You to heal Luke's hurt.

Luke returned every evening at dusk, ate the meal she'd prepared, then left the cabin while she cleaned up.

She always asked how his day had gone.

He had started to add a few words to his answer. "Saw a moose." "Stopped at a pretty waterfall for my lunch." "Found six cows and their calves enjoying a nice feed in a distant valley. Had to turn them back."

But still, he wouldn't look at her with any degree of friendliness.

Not that she was giving up.

. . .

Dark clouds had filled the sky all afternoon. She watched them twist and turn and hoped Luke would get back before it started to rain. The sky was heavy all afternoon without producing any rain. Pretend clouds. False promises.

She stared at the sky. Pretend. False. Like her.

She sat on the threshold of the cabin and rested her chin in her upturned hands. She hadn't meant to be false. Or so she'd told herself. Now she could see there was no excuse for what she'd done. Why hadn't she told him in her first letter that Tammy was writing for her? Let him decide if he was interested in her for who she was. Or told him straight out when he met her at the train station?

Because she was afraid that he'd reject her. And like she'd told him, she was desperate.

* * *

Luke watched the sky all afternoon. Several times he turned around, thinking he should ride back before he got soaked. Then at the thought of being shut in with Honor in that tiny space caused him to change his mind. Better to get wet than to have to face his feelings.

But he couldn't ride far enough, fast enough to outrun those feelings.

He cared for her despite his disappointment. What

was he to do? How could he listen to his heart when his mind constantly reminded him of her falseness?

It was near dark when he rode to the cabin. A cold breeze shivered up and down his spine. The rain still threatened but the clouds produced nothing.

He tended his horse and washed up in the cold water of the pump before he went to the house.

As always, she had a good meal waiting. Today there was a bouquet of flowers in a jug in the middle of the table. He squinted at it. How far had she wandered to gather those?

He gave a mental shrug. Let her do what she wanted. He'd not seen any sign of that bear again.

It was late and he was tired so stretched out on his bed as soon as Honor had finished cleaning the kitchen. She turned out the lamp and curled up under the table.

It stung his conscience to let her sleep there. But she made it clear she wouldn't take the bed. No point in letting a perfectly good bed go to waste.

Quiet descended upon them except for the wind moaning around the cabin.

Sleep came quickly.

A sharp sound jerked him from his slumber. He sat up in bed, trying to locate the source. It came again.

Honor.

Was she having a nightmare?

"Honor?"

She cried out again.

"Honor," he called her name louder.

It failed to awaken her.

He swung from the bed and reached under the bed to shake her. "Honor, wake up."

She whimpered and jerked away.

He didn't know if she was still in the throes of her dream or if she'd recoiled from his touch.

Unintelligible sounds came from her, and he decided she was still asleep. He scooted under the table and shook her harder. "Wake up."

She stiffened and gasped. And started to weep softly.

He eased himself out from under the table but didn't return to the bed. No matter how angry and disappointed he was with her, he couldn't abandon her to whatever feelings her dream had triggered, and he reached for her, drawing her to him.

She came readily.

He opened his arms and she clung to him. He shifted so he could lean against the bed and held her as she cried.

Her quiet sobbing ended but she didn't move from his embrace.

Nor did he want her to. His arms had ached for her every day since he'd learned of her trickery. Her nightmare had provided him an acceptable reason to hold her.

"I was dreaming." Her whispered words breathed against his chest.

"I'd say it was a nightmare." He waited but she didn't offer more. "Do you remember what it was?"

She nodded, her hair brushing his chin. "It's one I often have."

Again, he waited, hoping she would tell him more.

"In my dream, I am on my bed in the house where I lived with my aunt and uncle. I am awake. My covers disappear. The roof is missing. One by one all the walls are gone. I want to run away. Go where I'll be safe, but my shoes are gone and as I look for them, my bed disappears. I know it's only a dream and try to wake myself up. But I can't because in my dream, it's not a dream."

She trembled as she related the details of her nightmare, and he held her closer. He didn't need anyone to explain to him the significance of her dream. Since her earliest childhood she'd lived with not being welcomed; not feeling safe in her home.

On one level, he understood how that fear had driven her to desperate measures to get a permanent home. But he wanted to be more than a means to an end for her. He wanted to be enough.

Enough.

He'd never been enough.

His arms loosened and must have conveyed a message to Honor for she sat up.

"I'm sorry for waking you." She scooted over to the place on the floor where she'd slept. "Go back to bed. I'm all right."

He crawled under the sweet-smelling blankets and clutched them tight to his chest, but they did nothing to warm the place where Honor had laid her head. The cold emptiness of that spot echoed in his heart. He wanted more. But he didn't know what it looked like, how it felt or how to aim for it.

HE SLIPPED SILENTLY from bed the next morning. Honor still lay curled up under the table and he watched her for a moment. They had been so close to becoming husband and wife—at least in his mind. Now they were strangers and yet not. He couldn't say what they were.

Carrying his boots, he tiptoed from the room.

Outside, the sky was dark and lowering, threatening rain. He pulled on his boots and jogged to the barn to stand in the open doorway and study the clouds. He had no desire to ride in the rain even with a good slicker.

Or was he simply hoping for an excuse to stay here and—

And do what? It wasn't as if he wanted to spend the day with Honor.

Did he?

With a grunt of disgust, he saddled his horse and rode from the yard.

11

*A*t the sound of hoofbeats, Honor looked out the window in time to see Luke ride away. She stared after him. She'd thought things might have changed after her nightmare last night. He'd held her and comforted her as she told him the details. But he couldn't even wait for breakfast before he left.

Patience and prayer, she reminded herself. She would not give up nor lose hope.

The black clouds hid the mountains even though there were almost within touching distance, and they blocked out the sun.

The day matched her mood.

She filled the coffee pot just in case he returned and mixed batter for pancakes. Then she waited. The flowers she'd picked yesterday had wilted. She grabbed the jug holding them, went to the door, and tossed them out. No point in watching flowers with their heads hung down. It was too close to how she felt.

Needing something to do... anything to do... she went to the barn for a bucket and shovel and headed for the creek that was half a mile away. She'd been there before. In fact, that was where she'd found the flowers and picked them with such high hopes of seeing her connection with Luke improving.

She'd discovered a clay bank there and dug out enough to fill the bucket and carried it back to the cabin and got to work filling in the cracks between the logs. She should have started this task days ago if only to keep out creepy crawly bugs and flying insects.

The first pail full used up, she returned to the creek for more mud.

She was on her third bucket, standing on a chair to reach the higher areas when the door flew open startling her so much, she teetered.

"What are you doing?" Luke's question carried more than a touch of annoyance.

She sighed and got down. "Does everythin' I do stir your anger?" She didn't wait for a reply. "I'm chinkin' between the logs."

"I brought two rabbits for you to cook." He held out the skinned and dressed animals.

She wiped her hands on a damp cloth and took the meat. "I'll put them to stewing right away. Thanks." She took a large pot from the cupboard, put in the rabbits, covered them with water, added salt and pepper, and set the works on the stove.

"I wasn't angry." Luke still stood at the door.

"Sure sounded like it to me." She fussed over the stove as if it needed her attention when it didn't.

"It looked like you might fall."

"And you didn't want to have to tend me. I get it. But I've been takin' care of me a long time. Maybe all my life so you don't need to concern yerself." She was being petty, but she couldn't help it. Yes, this strain between them was her fault but she truly thought he'd understand.

"You'll have to excuse me if I'm a bit upset."

Assuming that he meant about her letter writing, she sighed. "I've explained why I did it. I was desperate."

"Guess a man would like to think he's more than a way to escape an unpleasant life. Maybe he'd like to think he's enough on his own."

Honor's hands stilled at his words. How was she to make him understand? "You with a big ranch, a loving family, a choice of homes, how can you begin to realize how it was for me? No parents. My aunt died. Despised and abandoned by my uncle. No job and no hope of getting' one." Her whispered words faded into painful silence.

He shifted as if about to take a step forward then reconsidered and leaned on the closed door. "I know more than you think."

At the way his voice deepened, his speech slowed she faced him. "What do you mean?"

He looked past her, his eyes full of darkness, his mouth a tight line then he sucked in air. "Remember I told you about riding the horse that wasn't quite ready?"

"When you got knocked out and your mother tended you?"

A smile flitted across his face then that harsh look returned. "I didn't tell you everything. I overhead Pa tell Ma that if he wanted something risky done, he'd ask me. But when he needed someone steady and reliable, he'd send Matt. He saw Matt as the better man."

The agony in Luke's voice tore a bloody path through Honor's heart and soul. She took a step forward.

He shook his head.

She bit her bottom lip to keep from protesting. All she wanted to do was comfort him, but he would not allow it. Instead, she turned back to the stove.

"I'll make breakfast." Though it was nigh on to noon.

"Fine. Gotta look after my horse." He was gone leaving her sniffing back tears.

By the time he returned, she had pancakes cooked, potatoes fried, and beans warmed. A combination breakfast and dinner.

He said grace and ate hurriedly. "Got to check on the west corner. Cows like to wander over there."

She handed him her mother's Bible before he escaped.

He gave her a look of patient acceptance and opened the pages. It seemed he was random in his choice of what to read. He cleared his throat. "That ye may be the children of your Father which is in heaven: for he maketh his sun to rise on the evil and on the good, and sendeth rain on the just and on the unjust.'" He closed the Bible. "Looks like we might get rain today."

She stared after him as he left the cabin.

The words of the verse had spoken to her, and she couldn't quite decide why. The evil and the good. Was she the former because of her sin? And yet God didn't withhold His gifts of sun and rain. And He forgave her. *Thank you, God. Please heal the rift between Luke and me.*

She cleaned up from the meal and returned to chinking.

Luke hadn't taken any food with him though it was possible he had some left from previous days. She chuckled. Possible but not likely. She'd seen the man eat.

She labored on the walls until late in the afternoon when she stepped back to see if she'd missed any spots. Nope. Every crack was filled. And her shoulders ached but she was satisfied with the work she'd done. No more feeling the wind coming in between the logs or worrying about bugs.

The stewing rabbit blessed the little house with a savory scent.

She would have liked to make another pie but wasn't about to risk meeting a bear or incurring Luke's anger so she opened a can of peaches and made a cobbler.

The room grew dark. It was early for that. She looked out the window. The clouds had lowered almost touching the roof. So heavy she couldn't imagine they wouldn't get a downpour.

She looked up the trail, hoping for a glimpse of Luke returning before he got soaked. She saw nothing, no one, and turned away. A watched pot never boiled. Likely a watched trail never revealed a rider either.

The cobbler cooled on the table. She'd added vegetables to the rabbit stew, and it was cooked. She lit the lamp to drive away the increasing darkness.

Rain pattered on the roof. She went to the window for the hundredth time. It was too dark, the rain too heavy for her to see past the hitching post.

She opened the door to look. Rain slashed against her and blocked her view, and she stepped back inside. The walls pressed in on her but there was no escape.

Where was Luke? Shouldn't he have come back, especially when it started to rain? What would she do if he was lost or hurt?

Luke had his rope around a cow and pulled. How did she manage to get herself stuck in the mud? It wasn't as if she couldn't have moved over a few feet and found clear water to drink. But no. She was too lazy to climb those few feet and now he was dealing with rain, mud, and frustration.

"Come on, you," he yelled loud enough to make his horse whinny a protest. He kicked his mount in the sides, and they pulled on the cow.

She bellowed.

Luke couldn't leave her, but he'd give anything to be out of this driving rain. He wore his slicker, but water trickled down his neck. He was cold. And hungry.

Finally, the cow got it into her head that he was trying to help and made an effort to aid her cause. Slowly her legs pulled from the muck. He didn't give her a chance to change her mind but yelled and pulled until she stood on dry ground.

And then was she grateful?

Not a chance. It was all he could do to get his rope off her without getting charged. He slapped her rear and sent her on her way.

"Ungrateful beast," he muttered as he coiled his lariat, wiped the mud from his boots, and turned toward home. Knowing a dry barn and a good feed awaited, his horse needed no urging.

Rain hid the trail from him, but the horse knew his way home and Luke ducked his head against the wet.

They rounded a familiar turn. The cabin should be right ahead. Yes. A light glowed from the window. Honor would have supper ready and the place warm.

He couldn't wait. Whether he meant to get in out of the rain, to enjoy a good meal, or to see Honor, he wasn't about to consider. Nor was he about to admit that seeing her might be as important to him as food and warmth.

He smiled to see her looking out the window as he rode past toward the barn. He took care of his horse's needs, washed the mud off at the pump then trotted toward the house.

The door opened before he got to it and Honor reached out to him.

He lifted his hands to stop her. "I'm wet and muddy."

She caught his hand and urged him forward. "And cold. Get in here." She undid the buttons on his slicker and helped him shrug out of it. She hung it, dripping, by the door. "Come and sit."

He dropped to the chair.

She bent over and pulled at his boots. She grunted and fell to her backside as one gave way. She rose and tackled the other.

He thought to stop her but was enjoying the attention too much.

The boots were off and put by the stove to dry, she grabbed a towel and rubbed his hair and neck.

He closed his eyes as a thousand longings and wishes raced through him. He couldn't take anymore and shifted away. "I'm fine."

"It will be a miracle if you don't catch your death of

a cold." She stepped back, her face wrapped in shock then she blinked. "Seems we're in need of a few miracles." Her voice dropped. "Or ya might say, answers to prayer."

He wondered if he'd heard her correctly but before he could ask her to repeat herself, she handed him a cup of coffee.

"Drink up. It'll warm yer innards."

He ducked to hide his smile. Her accent deepened when she was upset, and she was clearly upset. He let himself think it was worry over him.

She hustled about putting food on the table and sat across the corner from him.

He studied her flushed face, wondering at its cause. Then bowed his head.

For the first time in almost a week he was truly grateful. "Thanks, God, for food and rain and for that ornery cow getting out of the mud." He paused. It was on the tip of his tongue to say thanks for a woman to share his quarters with but there was too much unfinished business between them. Instead, he murmured, "Amen."

They dished up and he tucked into the food with a good appetite. She seemed less interested in the delicious food.

Was she feeling the unfinished business between them too?

If only he knew how to tackle the things hanging between them like wet sheets.

12

Honor's stomach was so jumpy she could hardly eat. Last night he'd held her... turning her insides to liquid honey. This evening she'd been so close, touching him in so many ways. Feeling his cold hands. Rubbing his damp hair. She closed her eyes and took a deep breath. How much more of this could she take before she embarrassed them both by begging for a kiss. And more.

He'd returned so late that they yawned and struggled to stay awake by the time they'd finished the meal. Which was a good thing. Going to their separate stations would give her a little distance.

She prepared to go outside to use the outhouse.

Seeing her intention, he lifted his slicker from the hook and draped it over her shoulders. Did she imagine that his hand lingered on her arm? No, it was only her own hungry heart imagining it.

She hurried down the path and into the darkness of the little building. She had to take off the slicker but took her time—inhaling his scent and his lingering warmth.

She might have stayed longer, alone with her thoughts and dreams, except for the smell and quickly made her way back to the house.

He lifted the raincoat from her and shrugged into it then stepped out into the darkness.

She hurriedly prepared for bed and was rolled up in her shawl when he returned.

He hung the slicker and sat on the bed to remove his boots.

She curled back further afraid he could see her.

He lifted a blanket from the bed and crawled to her side to spread it over her, every brush of his fingers creating a flash of awareness.

"I wish you weren't sleeping on the floor, but you should at least be warm."

"Thanks," she murmured around the thickness of her tongue.

She expected he'd return to the bed, but he stayed at her side. Her heart hammered against her ribs with hope, desperation, and uncertainty. Did he want to say more? Or forget about words and show her he cared with a kiss?

But he shuffled and sighed. "I don't understand why some young fellow back east didn't make you his wife."

Her heart jolted. "Are ya wishing someone had? Saved ya the trouble of dealing with me?"

"No." The word exploded from him. "I just find it hard to think someone hasn't snatched you up. You must have had plenty of beaus."

It was all she could do not to laugh. "I wasn't exactly a good catch. No money. Nothing of my own. And all these freckles."

"Any man would be proud to call you his wife."

A silence as deep as a pit followed his words. Did he not realize she was a wife? His wife? Would he ever be proud to acknowledge the fact? Sure didn't seem so. For a moment, she couldn't speak for fear of revealing the pain clogging her throat. But she didn't want him asking any more questions.

"What about you? You must have had lots of young ladies seeking yer attention."

He gave a mirthless chuckle. "You maybe didn't notice but there aren't a lot of young ladies in the area. Only know of a couple and they're no longer here."

Sensing there was more to his statement she pressed. "What happened to them?"

"Well, let's see. The preacher's daughter moved away. And the Luckhams' niece died in a train accident."

He might think he spoke calmly and perhaps he did, but she sensed something more in his tone.

"A train accident? That's awful." She shifted, wishing she could see his expression, but it was too dark. She could barely make out his outline. "Was she someone you were especially fond of?" The idea stung.

He shrugged, disturbing the blanket around her, and letting in cool air. "There was a time…."

When he seemed disinclined to continue, she prompted him. "Tell me about it." Even though the knowledge of a woman he mourned for would burn her insides.

His chest rose and fell. "We met her in the store. Matt and I. Matt was tongue-tied at her presence. She was very pretty, and we weren't used to conversing with a lady our age. It was me that introduced us and asked her about her trip. We found all sorts of excuses to return to the store. I was trying to come up with a way to go see her without Matt along, but he stuck like a bur." His chest rose and fell again as he sucked in air like he'd forgotten to breathe.

"One day Matt was gone. To town, Riley said. I was on my horse and on the road before he finished. My horse was lathered by the time I galloped down the street. Matt's horse was at the hitching rail. I clattered into the store. Only Mr. Luckham was there. He saw me and said Matt and Corine had gone for a walk. Said Matt had asked permission to court her, and he'd given it." He made a sound of disgust. "I sneaked down to the river to spy on them. They were courting all right." Bitterness colored his words. "I thought she cared for me like I cared for her. I loved her. Soon enough Matt announced they were to be married. She traveled home to make arrangements and then she was to return for their wedding." He stopped speaking and the pause lengthened.

She waited, not sure if he meant to say more or not.

"She was returning on the train when there was a crash." He swallowed audibly. "I can't believe that was four years ago."

Honor strained to hear his agonized words.

"Matt was devastated. So was I but I couldn't let anyone know that I'd also lost the woman I loved." He groaned. "I felt bad enough knowing I loved my brother's intended."

She felt his pain to the depths of her bones and reached for his hand, finding it in the dark and squeezing. "I'm sorry."

"I wasn't surprised that she chose him over me."

In those few words, she heard a wagonload of pain. She understood that he'd always felt he was in his twin's shadow. Matt was the responsible one. The favored one.

If only there was some way that she could make him understand that not everyone thought so.

"You're cold." She lifted the blanket and drew it across his body. "Let me warm you up." He didn't protest or leave when she left her arm across his chest.

The tension slowly eased from his body. Or was it the cold being replaced by the warmth of sharing the blanket? He shifted and covered her arm with his. His breath whispered out.

He didn't make a move toward returning to his bed. Rather, he moved into a position she assumed was more comfortable and tucked the blanket around her back.

She was afraid to breathe for fear of making him realize that he lay beside her, holding her against him. She closed her eyes and inhaled his scent—horse and grass and spicy soap. She allowed herself to enjoy the length of him against her. He was lean and muscled. His legs were so much longer than hers. If this was the only time that he'd hold her like this, she meant to gather every sensation, every scent, and feel to keep in her heart for the future.

Luke wakened, aware his hip pressed to the hard floor. And his arm lay across Honor as she curled against him, her back to his chest.

He smiled and stayed very still for fear of waking her. Her hair tickled his chin and he let it. It felt right to hold her like this. After all, they were husband and wife.

Yet not really.

Because she hadn't been honest about who she was.

Could he forgive her? Was he willing to? He considered the options. Forgive and be husband and wife. Don't forgive and be alone even though married.

All he'd wanted was someone like Gwen.

To be as good as his twin.

His mental wrangling was interrupted by the thud of a horse close to the cabin. He was certain he'd closed the barn doors well, but he scrambled from his warm cocoon and headed for the door.

"Hello, the house."

Visitors? Here? Or had a cowboy been sent to replace him so he could go home?

He wasn't sure he was ready for that. He had questions still needing answers. A quandary to resolve.

"Honor, someone's here." He didn't care for a stranger to see her all sleepy and dewy-eyed.

She jolted awake. He gave her a moment to get up before he went to the door.

A bearded man sat on a horse. A little boy peeked around the man. A loaded mule stood beside them. A mountain man. Or perhaps a miner.

"Good morning. Come on in. Join us for breakfast."

"Don't mind if I do." The man lowered the child to the ground and then swung off. "Name's Hob McCoy. This here is Kit." He held the boy's shoulder in his big hand. The comparison in the two was striking. The boy was thin to the point of starvation with hair almost white. His blue eyes darted from one thing to another. The man was big and brawny, with dark brown hair and a beard. Dark eyes that took in everything.

Honor joined Luke as he introduced himself. "And my wife, Mrs. Shannon."

"Mind if I water me animals?" Hob turned toward the pump.

"I'll help you." Luke accompanied the man to the trough. Brought out some oats for the animals while young Kit stayed so close to Hob that the man couldn't turn without stepping around him.

Luke admired the man's patience with the child.

Finished, they tied the animals to a post then Luke took Hob and Kit to the cabin.

The aroma of coffee filled the small space. The presence of a big man and a small child made it feel crowded. He wondered where everyone would sit.

"Mr. Hob, you and Kit sit on the bench." Honor indicated where she meant. She indicated Luke should take the chair. "You go ahead. I'll eat later."

Every nerve in his body protested her acting like a servant even if she'd been in the role many times. She was his wife, for goodness' sake. But perhaps she was right. There wasn't room for them all nor plates enough.

She put cups of coffee before the men. "Would you like some water?" she asked the boy.

He nodded, his gaze barely touching her before he lowered his head to stare at his plate.

She set a tin cup of water before him and brought a plate of pancakes.

Luke spoke before his guests could reach for food. "I'll ask the blessing."

Hob gave him a surprised look then ducked his

head. He couldn't say what Kit did because he closed his eyes to pray.

Luke admired the amount of food Hob devoured. Luke figured the only thing that stopped him was there was nothing left to eat. Kit had barely eaten enough to keep a mouse alive.

"Thanks to the missus for the good breakfast. We dinna often eat so good, do we, Kit?"

The boy shook his head.

"Where're you off to?" Luke expected they were heading higher up.

"Gots me a mine up there." Hob pointed vaguely to the west. "Best be on our way." He looked into his empty cup. "Less'en there's more coffee in that there pot?"

Honor sprang up from her place on the edge of the bed and brought the pot, filling both Hob and Luke's cups.

Silent as a shadow, Kit slipped outside.

Hob watched him go. "The mountain's no place for a boy."

Luke considered the boy's circumstances. "Must be lonely for him."

"Ain't good for him a'tall."

"His mother?" Luke prompted.

"I buried her this spring. Boy ain't hardly spoke since. Not that he's a bother, mind ya." He looked from Luke to Honor with interest. "He ain't my kin. I took up with his ma three years ago and she brought him along. Near as I can figger he's nigh unto six years old."

Luke wondered why Hob was telling him all this. A glance at Honor and he guessed she wondered the same thing.

"Kit's a good boy. No problem a'tall. But he needs family. A ma and pa." Hob's study on Luke and Honor was long and considering. Then he pushed from the table. "Thank ye for the feed. Best be on my way."

Luke followed him outside. Hob and Kit mounted up and rode away heading up the trail deeper into the mountains. He reasoned they would disappear there, and he'd never see them again. He watched until they were out of sight then returned to the cabin.

"They're gone."

"I feel for that little boy. He sort of reminds me of myself." Honor looked beyond him. Whether her gaze was following the departed riders or seeing something of her past, he couldn't say.

"At least Hob didn't seem unkind." Her emotion-filled eyes met Luke's.

He wished he could offer reassurance. "I'm sure the boy will be all right." There was no way he could tell, and Honor knew it.

She gave a fleeting smile that informed him of that fact.

"I just realized it's Sunday. We don't do unnecessary work on the Lord's Day. What would you like to do?" The words were out of his mouth before he remembered he was angry at her. All he could think was he wanted to enjoy the day with her.

Her eyes brightened. "What would you suggest?"

"If you're up to riding we can go to that little waterfall I found."

"I'd love that. Give me a few minutes to put together a lunch." She stopped. "It's all right to take a picnic?"

"It's perfect." Except for her hesitation. And that was his fault. If only they could undo a few things.

He left her to prepare food for the outing and went to saddle the horses.

Was he willing to forgive her? Or was his pride getting in the way?

Why did Matt always come out of things as the better man? The favored one?

Why was Luke the one who learned to make the best of things?

Honor was a good woman. She'd make a good wife.

But she wasn't like Gwen and that's what he'd had in mind.

13

*H*onor gathered up food for a picnic. If she'd had a little warning, she could have made it more special. But for her, it wasn't the food that mattered. It was that Luke had invited her to go with him. Did that mean he forgave her? She might never replace this Corine in his affections, but she'd make him a good wife. One he could be pleased with. *Please, God, let it be so.*

Hearing his return, she took the sack and stepped out to greet him.

She hadn't been on her horse since they'd arrived at the cabin but neither the lingering moisture in the air nor the memory of her sore body from her previous ride could put a damper on her eagerness.

He cupped his hands to help her into the saddle. He lingered at her side, as if wanting to say something, then patted her leg and went to his own horse.

"It's not a long way."

She didn't answer. Because the only words she that came to her mind were that she'd be happy to ride day and night if it kept her with him, especially if he would speak kindly to her.

They rode side by side up the trail where he'd gone every day. After riding ten minutes, he turned right, and the route grew steeper and more narrow. She was forced to fall behind him.

He shifted to look back at her. "Holler if you have any problems."

"Will do." On the ride to the cabin, he hadn't once turned to check on her. This concern was a welcome change. Her lungs could barely hold the deep, grateful breath she sucked in.

They rode for a spell, the only sound was the clop of horse hooves, the creak of the saddle, and cheerful bird song.

He stopped and signaled her forward. She crowded to his side.

"You can see the waterfall from here." He pointed through the trees.

She saw flashing water like silver dancers on rocks and told him.

He grinned.

"And so many birds singing." She sought them in the branches. Saw a sparrow-looking one.

"Yup. Birds are always cheerful." He seemed amused more than interested.

"Guess that's so. Maybe we should learn a lesson from them."

He considered her. "What lesson would that be?"

"Ignore the mud. Enjoy the sun." She nodded wisely, hoping he would think of things more practical to people. She had something specific in mind. Ignore the wrongs, enjoy the good. She meant herself.

He looked at the trees and laughed. "Maybe we *should* be more like the birds. It might be nice to fly."

She wasn't sure if he was teasing her or misunderstood. And perhaps on purpose. Being with him on this outing left her a little unsettled. Was he willing to overlook her falseness in letting Tammy write the letters or not?

He flicked his reins and they moved on, making their way through trees that clung to the trail and then they reached a grassy bank. Straight ahead, water fell merrily over rocks.

"What a soothing sound and a whole orchestra of birds." Her voice revealed only a touch of the awe she felt at the beauty of nature.

"I thought you might like it." He dismounted and then helped her down.

Was it her imagination or did his hands linger at her waist? She was willing to believe his gaze was warm and inviting.

The horses shuffled taking his attention and he led them to green grass to graze.

He brought the sack of food with him and put it on

a table-high rock then reached for her hand. "Come on, let's explore."

She laughed for no other reason than it felt good to have him this way. She would have followed him up a cliff if he'd asked it of her.

But they only climbed the grassy hill to the top of the falls. The water ran down a series of rocks like descending a staircase. There was something fascinating about watching the water and they sat on the bank to enjoy it.

She looked around. "It's so peaceful."

"I know. Kind of makes a person forget his troubles."

Her gaze went to him as he pulled blades of grass and ran his thumbnail along them, splitting each in two. He seemed absorbed in the process.

Then he tossed away the latest blade and leaned back to look at her. "I don't want to be at odds with you."

"Nor I with you." Her words whispered from a grateful, overflowing heart. "I regret not being honest with you from the start." She shrugged. "I reasoned that once I proved that I was a good wife and homemaker, you wouldn't care if I could read and write." Corine was no doubt well educated. It was foolish to be jealous of a deceased woman, but she was and struggled to take a breath as she waited for his reply.

"You're a good cook and a good homemaker. I'm grateful."

Of course, he hadn't said she was a good wife. That was yet to be proven. "Thank you."

He pulled her closer, dipped his head, and kissed her. It was a quick brushing of their lips that left her aching for more. More than acceptance as cook and cleaner. She wanted to be adored.

She picked a blade of grass and ran her finger along it, keeping her head down lest he see the longing in her face.

He shifted to study their surroundings. "Isn't it strange that it's hard to see the mountains when we're right in them?"

She looked around. "I see what you mean. They say you can't see the forest for the trees. Seems you can't see the mountains for the rocks."

He laughed at her observation. "I've something more to show you." He pulled her to her feet and kept hold of her hand as he led her through the birches. They were climbing enough to make her breathless and then they broke into the open. The ground fell away before them to a turquoise lake below and across from it, a rugged gray and blue peak, with a necklace of green pines.

She stared in wonder and disbelief. "It's amazing."

He draped an arm across her shoulders and no longer was the scene the only amazing thing. Her feelings for this man more than rivaled it.

He dipped his head to hers. "Ma loved the mountains. She said they were a constant reminder of God's power and love. She used to quote a verse from the Bible, 'As the mountains are round about Jerusalem, so the Lord is round about his people from henceforth even for ever.'"

"I like that. Do you know where it's found?"

"Can't say as I do. Maybe the Psalms. Why?"

Shame and embarrassment left her momentarily tongue-tied. But she didn't mean to hide the truth about who and what she was from him any longer. "I'd like to find it and read it for myself. That way I can memorize it."

"You've done this before, I think."

She turned toward him. They were so close she could see the golden flecks in his pupils, and she held his gaze as she murmured the words of the verse she'd learned by heart. "'The steadfast love of the Lord never ceases; his mercies never come to an end; they are new every morning, great is your faithfulness.'"

"I read that one morning, didn't I?"

She nodded.

"How did you find it?"

"I saw about where you'd opened the Bible and I just began looking for it. It's in a book that starts with an L and has a long name."

"Lamentations."

"I'll take your word for it." Now she'd know how to say it. She tucked the knowledge into her head.

Chuckling softly, he pulled her into his arms. "I'm not sure what to think of you."

It was all she could do not to stiffen. "Why?"

"Because you aren't what I expected."

Her heart clenched so painfully that she almost cried out. "Because I can't read or write?"

"Not just that." He seemed to consider his words. "It's because you are you."

"What's that supposed to mean?" It didn't sound very promising in her mind.

"You're a fighter and yet kind and cheerful."

"Oh."

"Yes, I'm beginning to appreciate who you are."

That sounded nice. "I appreciate who you are too." So much so that she couldn't resist any longer and leaned closer, lifting her face and capturing his surprised lips with hers.

His surprise disappeared and he deepened the kiss.

They broke apart.

Her eyes felt too wide. Her breath stuttered from her. And if she wasn't mistaken, he felt the same.

Was this the beginning of their moving forward? Truly husband and wife?

* * *

Luke held Honor in his arms. His heart thundered in his chest. They'd kissed and it had about knocked his boots off. What did it mean? Was it simply that he was a man and she a woman? That, as his wife, he had every right to kiss her and enjoy her sweet lips? Or was it more? Yes, he was learning to appreciate her strengths. Was that enough? Could he make second-best work?

He shifted. He'd always been second best. Seems he should be used to it. And know how to deal with it.

Although he barely moved, she must have sensed his withdrawal for she looked up at him, her eyes wide and uncertain. "Is there something wrong?"

"Nope." And right then and there, without even really thinking about it, he decided he might as well make the best of the situation. "Look." He turned her toward the scene below them. "Can you see them?" Half a dozen deer crept from the trees and tiptoed to the edge of the water.

"Yes." Her answer was barely a whisper.

They watched as the animals dipped their heads to drink then slipped back into the trees and out of sight.

"'Tis a wonderful country."

He smiled. "You won't get an argument from me on that score." He tucked her against his side, prepared to stay there as long as she was willing, enjoying the scenery and her. Mostly her.

But eventually, she sighed. "Thank you for showing me this and..."

He waited but she didn't finish. "What else?"

She lifted her face to him. "For forgiving me."

The whispered words struck his heart.

Her eyes were wide and searching. "You have, haven't you?"

"I suppose I have."

Her smile filled her face making him feel like he'd given her a magnificent gift. Forgiveness felt good.

"Are you hungry?" he asked.

"A little. Hob didn't leave much breakfast for anyone else."

They laughed together at acknowledging the appetite of the big man.

She sobered. "Kit is awfully thin, don't you think?"

"I thought so too. But I'm sure Hob feeds him."

"Maybe he's mourning his ma. Poor little boy." She rocked her head back and forth. "Like Hob said, living in the mountains isn't good for a child."

"He'll grow up to be a mountain man, I suppose." He could see that his words failed to ease Honor's concerns about Kit. Not that they were any comfort to him either. Hob was right in saying the boy needed a family. "But at least Hob seems kind."

They reached the place where he'd left the sack of food and she opened it to reveal biscuits, cheese, and cookies that she spread out on a red-checkered cloth.

He raised his eyebrows at the cloth. "That was in the cabin?"

She chuckled. "I think someone mistook it for a drying towel."

"It makes this a special occasion."

"It isn't the cloth that makes this occasion special." She looked hard at him.

He understood her meaning. She meant his

forgiveness. But he didn't acknowledge that. "No, sharing a picnic with my wife makes it special." Her pleased smile was his reward.

Their gazes held like a tender hug. He sought something from her, but he didn't even know what it was. Her smile would do for now.

He bowed to pray. His heart overflowed with gratitude, but he couldn't think of how to put his feelings into words. "Heavenly Father, maker of heaven and earth. Your creation is beautiful, and we thank You for it. I want to thank You for Honor too. And for the food. Amen."

Honor remained with her head bowed.

"Did I offend you?"

Her head came up, her eyes blazing blue. "You thanked God for me."

"You needn't sound so surprised."

She shrugged. "Well, I am."

He reached over and touched her chin. "Don't be." If not for the rock between them that served as a table, he would kiss her.

Her gaze lowered to his lips. Was she thinking the same thing?

He shifted around the rock until he could pull her into his arms.

She readily lifted her face to him, and readily met him halfway for a kiss. She sighed and leaned into him.

He pressed his cheek to her hair. They could make

this work.

They turned their attention to the food. Everything tasted better than it had in the past. Must be because he shared it with his wife. *His wife.* He was truly married. Maybe it was time to make it a true union.

If she was ready and willing.

They lingered over the picnic. When every crumb was gone, they put the cloth back in the sack.

They wandered up and down the side of the waterfall. The sound of running water was a perfect backdrop for their conversations.

She told him about caring for her sick aunt. "Sometimes she was too weak to even say thank you." She didn't talk about her uncle directly, but he caught hints of the man's meanness.

Wanting to put the conversation on a better note, he asked, "What is your favorite memory?"

"Ohh that's a hard one. I felt safe at the Johansens. I got treated well. That's where I learned my letters." Her voice lowered. "Almost learned to read and write."

"Seems to me you do both. Didn't you say you found that verse in the Bible and read it? Didn't you write to your friend?"

"It's not much."

He pulled her to him. "It's better than nothing. Now tell me more good things you remember."

"Once I discovered a flower growing in the path from Uncle's house to the back shed. Just a dandelion but I thought it was very brave and stubborn to poke up through the hard clay."

He watched a sweet smile curve her lips. "I think you learned to see the good and the beauty around you despite adverse circumstances."

"Maybe I did." Her eyes danced with an appreciation of his words. Then her mouth made an O. "I know my best memory. It was when Tammy joined the Abernathy household. She'd been attending a school but had finished and came to live with her sister. She often visited in the nursery."

Luke realized Tammy had been a very good friend to Honor. Even if she'd encouraged Honor's dishonesty.

Honor continued, "I guess the best day I spent with her was the time she invited me to accompany her to a circus. I'm sure people seeing us together would assume I was her maid, but she didn't treat me like that, you know?"

"I'm glad she was good to you."

"Me too." Her gaze went past him into the distance. Perhaps into her memories. "We laughed at so many things. A juggler who pretended to drop the balls he juggled then pretended to trip as he recovered them. The house of mirrors. First, I was so fat." She held her hands out to indicate how large the mirror had made her and puffed out her cheeks. "Then I was skinny." She pressed her hands to her sides and sucked in her cheeks. "Then I had no legs."

He joined her in laughter.

She sobered and continued, "We watched animals performing in the big tent. She bought me hot dogs and cotton candy and an ice cream sundae. We wandered home later in the day. Parted ways at the gate."

He wondered why the joy in her voice had deepened to something else.

"I paused at the end of the street and stared at Tammy's house. It was a fine house, but that wasn't what pulled at my heart. It was the idea of a home where one belonged and was welcome."

She ducked her head but not before he caught the pain that flashed through her eyes.

She had stepped away and he reached for her and pulled her close as she continued. "I guess all I've ever wanted was a home like that. Didn't matter the size. What mattered was the feeling." She gave him a direct look. "What counts is the welcome within."

"Honor, you will always have a home where you are welcome." He meant it with his whole heart.

"Thank you." She hugged him so hard his ribs protested but he didn't say anything.

They spent the afternoon sharing stories of their past. He told her of the move to Montana his family had made when he was thirteen. "We drove our herd of cows with us. I liked best when I was the one who did the night watch with Pa."

"I'm guessing you were very good at that."

"I hadn't thought of it, but Pa often picked me." He recalled something. "Pa said I didn't seem nervous in the dark."

"Seems like your pa was thankful for your help."

"Maybe so." It was something to consider. That his pa might have chosen him.

The sun dipped toward the west, and they returned to the horses.

He was reluctant to end the day but... "We need to get back before dark."

She moved closer to him. "It's been a nice day. Perhaps the best I've ever had. All thanks to you."

He trailed his finger along her cheek, caught her chin, and bent to kiss her.

The kiss ended and she rested her head on his shoulder.

With a sigh, he shifted. "Let's go home, Mrs. Shannon."

His hand lingered on her leg as he helped her adjust in the saddle. They rode side by side when the trail allowed. When she had to fall behind because there wasn't room for two horses, he felt deprived. He smiled to think how his thoughts had changed from bitter to blessed.

Must be the power of forgiveness.

They were almost back to the cabin, riding side by side. He wanted to explain how he felt but couldn't think of the right words.

Maybe if he just said what he was feeling...

But before anything came to his tongue, he pulled up and stared. "Someone's at the cabin." Sitting on the doorstep as if waiting for their return. Anyone would know it was acceptable to go inside. Doors were left unlocked in this area. If a person needed shelter or food, it was available.

He squinted and blinked, trying to clear his vision. But nothing changed. "It's Kit. What is the boy doing here?" Luke looked around. There was no sign of Hob.

14

Honor guessed the boy had been abandoned. Her gut had warned her that the boy needed a home. Hob, himself had suggested it. She knew all the signs and yet she'd done nothing. She could have offered to take the boy. Of course, she would need Luke's permission to do so.

Luke moved ahead but she stayed put. He pulled up when he saw she didn't move forward.

"Something wrong?" He studied her face and must have read the feeling she couldn't hide. Didn't want to hide.

"I told you he reminds me of myself."

"Because he's an orphan?"

"No. Because Hob doesn't want to take care of him."

Luke looked at the boy and then back at Honor. "I thought he seemed fond of the boy. I didn't tell you, but Kit was underfoot when we tended Hob's animals and Hob never seemed fussed about it."

"I think he cared for the boy, but Kit isn't his. And remember he said the mountains weren't a good place for a child?" Her attention returned to Kit who sat with his chin in his upturned hands. "I want to believe he is acting out of concern for the boy." Not simply anxious to be shed of the care of a child. She couldn't allow her own experience to cloud her thinking and yet she couldn't help it.

Luke studied Honor and then turned back to considering Kit. "Maybe we're jumping to conclusions. Let's go find out what's going on." They rode to the cabin.

Kit rose and waited for them; his face was almost expressionless except Honor recognized the signs. His eyes were too wide. His hands curled tightly.

"Howdy," Luke called as he dismounted and helped Honor to the ground.

"Hello."

No mistaking the tremor in Kit's voice. Honor glanced at Luke to see if he'd noticed. He gave a barely-there nod indicating he had before he turned his attention back to the boy.

"Where's Hob?" Thankfully, there was no sharpness in Luke's tone. Nothing to frighten Kit.

"Gone."

"When's he coming back?" Luke and Honor stood

side by side, not approaching Kit. She understood how skittish he would be. Seems Luke did too.

"He's not."

"What do you mean?" Luke's quiet tone continued.

"He sent me back. Said I was to stay with yous." The poor child could hardly get the words out.

Recognizing and knowing the terror that would grip his heart, and tighten his lungs, Honor paused only long enough to send a silent question to Luke.

He understood and gave his answer. "Of course, you can stay with us."

Thank you, Luke. She eased toward the child, taking her time. She squatted to his eye level. "We'd be so happy to have a boy like yourself. Won't we, Luke?" She glanced back to see him nod.

Kit studied her face a good long moment then shifted to consider Luke. "You want a boy?"

She touched his shoulder. He shivered beneath her palm. "Not just any boy. Only you." The words she'd longed to hear all her life came easily. "You willing to be our boy?"

His eyes brightened. The tension in his shoulders eased enough for her to feel it. He nodded.

Luke moved forward and put his hand on Kit's other shoulder. "Then it's settled. Welcome to our family."

Tears clogged the back of Honor's throat. *Welcome to our family.* Words that meant as much—if not more—to her as they did to Kit.

LINDA FORD

She stood and hugged Luke with one arm, pulling Kit close with the other. He was stiff but she sensed the hunger in the boy's heart.

A hunger she meant to do everything she could to satisfy.

They remained in an awkward three-corner hug for several seconds then broke apart.

"How long have you been waiting here?" she asked.

He shrugged.

"I'm guessing you're hungry." Of course, he was. She expected he was always hungry. Always afraid. "I'll have something ready shortly."

"Why don't you come and help me with the horses?" Luke waited for the boy to decide to do so, and Honor watched them walking side by side to the barn.

Tears stung her eyes. A husband. A child. A home. Home was wherever the other two were. *Thank you, God.*

She started a fire in the stove. There was no meat, but she'd previously cooked a pot of beans. She quickly mixed together the ingredients for Johnny cake. A growing boy needed vegetables and the garden back at the ranch offered plenty. Not that she was eager to go back. She and Luke had mended things, but they had a long way to go yet.

The table was set, the food was ready when Luke and Kit returned. Luke ushered the boy in ahead of him. Kit stood stiff, waiting for instructions.

A familiar tightness caught at Honor's insides. She knew she could change things for Kit.

Suddenly she realized a powerful truth. By helping Kit, she could heal her own painful wounds.

By the dampness of Kit's hands and hair, she knew Luke had instructed him to wash at the pump along with him. "Kit, you can sit here." She indicated the end of the bench closest to Luke. She would sit on Kit's other side, the boy between them.

Luke said grace and then the food was passed.

Kit took only a small spoonful of beans and the tiniest piece of Johnny cake.

Honor lifted her gaze to Luke, silently asking if the boy shouldn't eat more? Should they encourage it?

"Kit, there's plenty of food here." Luke took the pot of beans and added a scoop to Kit's plate. He put on another piece of Johnny cake.

Kit looked up at Luke, studying him for several seconds and then turned to Honor.

She understood his uncertainty. "Go ahead and eat." Hob might not have been cruel and miserly like her uncle, but Kit was far too familiar with uncertainty. She didn't start eating until Kit picked up his fork and tackled his meal.

Supper over, the three of them rose.

"While I do up the dishes, why don't you two find a blanket for Kit?" She hoped there was something in the barn or storeroom though she'd not seen anything.

Kit jumped up. "I gots one." He was out the door in

an instant and returned carrying a worn gunny sack that he lowered to the floor. He pulled out a bundle. "Me bedroll."

It looked far from adequate but this time of year he didn't need much.

"Where I put it?" He stood waiting like a statue.

Honor waited for Luke to answer. When he didn't immediately respond, Kit turned to leave. "I sleep in barn. That okay."

Honor caught him. "No, it's not okay. You heard Luke. We're family now. You'll sleep in here with us."

Finally, Luke found his voice. "Put your bed roll wherever you like."

The boy looked around then crawled under the table and spread his thin blankets.

Honor stared at the bedding. Where was she going to sleep? She swallowed hard. What was wrong with her? There was room for another person on the floor.

She would not look at the narrow bed nor remember the hope she'd had that she and Luke would truly reconcile and become man and wife.

She wouldn't be comfortable doing so with a child nearby.

Would Luke be regretful of the situation or—

She couldn't bring herself to look at him for fear of what she'd see.

Perhaps his thoughts differed from hers. He might be glad of an excuse to not invite her to share his bed.

* * *

Luke could hardly find his voice. To think that Kit expected they wanted him to sleep in the barn. To live with the knowledge that the only person he knew had left him behind. To witness his reluctance to eat. They all scoured at his insides until he felt raw.

Nor did he overlook the fact that much of Honor's life had been like this. His heart cracked and bled as he realized he'd treated her almost as badly as her uncle had. Judging her and condemning her for things she couldn't help such as her lack of education and purposely overlooking those things that mattered— her strength in overcoming the challenges in her life, how pleasant and lovely and helpful she was.

He would have gathered them both in his arms and he would do so at every opportunity, but they needed more than that. They needed security. A home. And love.

Words he'd heard his mother speak sprang to his mind. One of his brothers had asked her what love was. Most likely Riley seeing as he was the oldest and at that time probably had a gal he was interested in.

"Love," she said, "Is more than a feeling. It's putting someone's needs ahead of your own. It's wanting what's best for them even if it costs you something. It's a decision to put them first."

He remembered how her gaze had gone to Pa. "It's

overlooking little things that annoy. And concentrating on the good the other person offers."

Luke knew that Pa often overlooked Ma's needs.

He did not want to be like his father. He would do his best to be like his mother.

And he'd start right now. He carried the dishes to the basin of water. He handed a drying towel to Kit. "I'll wash. You dry while Honor puts things away."

Kit's face wrinkled in uncertainty.

Honor opened her mouth.

Guessing she meant to protest, Luke spoke before she could voice her words. "We're a family. We work together."

She closed her mouth and collected the serving dishes then put away the remaining food.

He smiled as he washed the few dishes. He'd seen the happy look on her face and congratulated himself on pleasing her.

They finished at the same time. He emptied out the water. Honor showed Kit how to hang the towel behind the stove to dry.

He thought of suggesting they go for a walk before bed, but he had a better idea. "Who'd like to hear a story?"

Honor's eyes flashed. "You'd read to us?"

"If you'd like."

"I'd like it very much. How about you, Kit?"

He nodded.

Luke pulled the book from his saddlebags where they hung by the door.

Honor watched. "Do you always carry a book with you?"

"Never know when you'll have to hole up someplace. A book helps pass the time." He sat crossways on the cot and patted the space beside him. "Come and sit with me."

Kit hesitated but Honor urged him along. The boy ended up pressed between the two of them. And to Luke that seemed the best possible place he could be and not just to listen to a book being read.

He opened to the first page and began to read. "'Robinson Crusoe. Chapter One. Robinson's Family— His Elopement from His Family. I was born in the year 1631, in the city of York, of a good family, though not of that country…'"

It was one of his favorite books and it pleased him to see both the others mesmerized by the story. He read several chapters until his voice grew hoarse and then he slowly closed the book.

"Look," Honor whispered. "He's fallen asleep."

Kit's head lulled against her shoulder, his eyes closed and his mouth slightly ajar.

She eased away from him and lay him on the cot.

He got up and lifted the boy's feet to the bed.

Honor covered him with a blanket, and they stood watching him sleep. She caught Luke's hand and squeezed it. He squeezed back.

"Come outside with me," he whispered, and they tiptoed from the room.

She didn't give him a chance to speak. "Did you mean it when you said he could stay with us?"

"Every word."

Her eyes were midnight blue and intense in the dimming light, searching his heart and soul. He let her do so. Let her see he was sincere.

Finally, she gave a tiny nod and he let out the breath he'd been holding.

"Good." Her voice might have carried warning as well as approval. "He needs a lot of assurance."

"I know. What can we do to help him?"

"Just be here for him. Always."

"I can do that. I know you can too."

They moved slowly along the path to the barn and stopped there. He wanted to promise he'd do everything he could for her as well as Kit.

She stared at the cabin. "What if he wakes up and we're gone?"

He could have said that Kit had likely been left alone many times, but he wanted something different for the boy. Kit should have complete confidence that they would always be there for him.

They returned to the cabin.

Kit lay on the floor wrapped in his thin blanket. He was right against the cot.

He opened his eyes when they entered. "Bed for the mama and papa."

Honor stiffened.

Luke caught her arm and leaned close to whisper. "I think he needs to see us together." It was the perfect reason to get her to share his bed even if having a child sleeping beside them would make certain they would do nothing more than sleep. Even knowing the limitations, he couldn't wait to hold her in his arms.

She studied the bed a moment then slipped off her shoes and stretched out on the edge closest to the boy.

Luke tugged his boots off in record time, tossed them to the middle of the floor, and crawled in between Honor and the wall. He pulled the blanket up and tucked it around them both.

"It's more comfortable than the floor," he whispered.

"It's a mite crowded."

Her face was away from him and she, too, whispered but he heard every syllable. Told himself he also heard a thread of regret and would believe only that she wished things were such they could better enjoy their time together. Back home, they would have a much wider bed to share. And Kit would be in his own room.

Luke draped his arm across Honor and felt her stiffen. "Relax. The boy needs to know we're a family." In every sense of the word. But that time would come. He believed it with his whole heart.

Her breathing deepened. She shuffled around into a more comfortable position, and he smiled. They had gotten off to a rocky start, but they could make this work.

No, she wasn't Gwen. But she had her good points.

He fell asleep before he could name them. He started awake to an unfamiliar sound. He was ready to scramble out of bed when Honor caught his hand.

"It's Kit. He shouted in his sleep. He rolled over. I think he's still sleeping."

He settled back beside her. "He sounded scared."

"Nightmares can be unsettling. I'll ask him about it in the morning. Now go to sleep." A yawn muffled her words.

"Bossy," he murmured quietly; not caring if she heard.

"Just tired."

He was too but sleep eluded him for a long time. He was married but not yet a husband. And now he was a father to a child not his own.

Life sure did take strange twists.

LUKE WOKE EARLY the next morning and lay very still. He eased his arm off Honor, hoping to slip out to the barn without disturbing the others but she stirred as soon as he moved. She turned toward him, all dewy-eyed and kissable.

He leaned over and brushed his lips to hers.

She sighed and brought her hands up to pull him closer.

Kit sat up, yawned, and stretched.

Luke groaned. Any thought of lingering in bed and making love to his wife was squelched. He slipped from the cot and pulled on his boots very aware of Honor's gaze following his every move.

"Come on, Kit." He and the boy left the cabin. They took their turns at the outhouse and then went to the barn. He had to patrol the borders of the ranch, but it meant leaving Kit and Honor behind. He shrugged. Seems that's what ordinary family life meant except there was nothing ordinary about his family.

He grinned. Wouldn't Matt be surprised to see he'd added a boy to his family?

Kit followed, silent as a shadow, while Luke did the chores.

The animals were fed and watered, the one horse put out to graze in the small, fenced pasture when Honor called them for breakfast.

"You hungry?" he asked the boy.

Kit nodded, not quite meeting Luke's eyes then looked toward the cabin. The longing Luke saw on the boy's face sucked the saliva from his mouth. This child needed love and security. His gaze went to the cabin. Perhaps not unlike Honor.

Luke crossed his arms as if that could hold back his sense of failure. He should have never made her feel that he rejected her. Even if she wasn't what he'd asked for and expected.

Kit glanced at him, waiting for Luke to make the first move toward the cabin.

"Race ya."

Kit looked surprised. Then he giggled and headed for the cabin.

Luke let him get a head start and then thundered after him. By the time they reached the doorway, they were both laughing as was Honor.

They sat down to a good meal. They were going through supplies faster than he'd planned. He'd go hunting this morning before he went to patrol the ranch's borders.

Kit ate better today than yesterday.

Luke liked to think that he and Honor had something to do with that.

The food was gone, and he reached for Honor's Bible. "Kit, do you know about God and the Bible?"

His eyes were wide. He didn't answer. Perhaps he was too young to remember. Luke had been reading from random places in the Bible but decided it was time to be more deliberate and he opened to the first page and began to read. Every time he read, 'God saw it was good,' he glanced at Honor, and they shared a smile. He finished the chapter and closed the book.

"I'll bring in some meat before I go check on the cows." He pushed from the table.

Kit was immediately on his feet. "I go with you."

"I thought you'd want to stay here."

Kit shook his head hard enough to whip his hair around his face. "I go with you."

Luke looked to Honor for her reaction. She seemed as startled as he. Then she shrugged.

"I suppose he's used to riding with Hob."

"Very well." Luke thought it a boring way to spend a day and knew that Kit's legs would get tired of sitting astride. But the boy followed him. Luke swung into the saddle and reached down to pull Kit up behind him.

Honor watched from the doorway and called goodbye to them.

Luke waved. "See you later."

Kit waved and echoed the words.

It didn't take long for Luke to find two rabbits. Kit hunkered down beside him as he dressed the animals. He followed on Luke's heels as Luke carried them to the horse and hung them from the saddle. They returned to the cabin to deliver the meat.

"Do you want to stay here?" Perhaps the boy had changed his mind.

"I go with you."

Very well. They again called out *see you later* and he headed his horse up the trail. He passed where he'd turned to take Honor to the waterfall.

Was that really only yesterday? Life sure had changed in a few short hours.

They rode in silence, Kit clinging to Luke's back. They reached a draw where Luke had found cows before. A handful of them had discovered this narrow draw and returned to it over and over. They were there again today. He'd leave them to enjoy the grass except the valley led into a rocky, rugged area where it would take several men and hours of work to get animals back to ranch property.

The cows didn't want to leave, and Luke and his horse were given a workout of sharp turning and sudden stops before they were all headed the right way.

A few times he feared he might lose Kit in the quick twists, but the boy clung to Luke's shirt with fisted hands.

They settled into a steady walk behind the cows.

Luke looked back to Kit. "You hung on good."

Kit's eyes were solemn.

"Were you scared?"

Kit's eyes widened and, if Luke wasn't mistaken, held a gleam. He shook his head.

Luke laughed. "So you like a little adventure, do you?"

Kit grinned.

Luke grinned too as he turned back to his task. He liked a boy with spunk. It reminded him a bit of himself. And despite what his father had said about him being rash at times Luke liked the idea of having a boy like himself.

When the cows were far enough away, they might hesitate to return to the enticing valley, Luke turned back. He dismounted and lifted Kit from the saddle then shared with him the lunch Honor had prepared.

Kit ate slowly as if savoring every morsel which, Luke decided, wasn't such a bad thing.

They drank from the nearby stream, then rather than hurry on his way, he and Kit wandered along the edge of the water. Kit picked up a rock, examined it, and put it in his pocket.

Luke squeezed the boy's shoulder. He could remember collecting rocks. In fact, there might still be some in the dresser drawer in his old bedroom in the big house where Andy now lived. The house Pa had built and where Ma and the boys had lived.

They returned to the horse, and he rode to the west. They saw a handful of cows drifting too far away and moved them down the slope. But other than those few, they saw nothing but rocks and trees and gurgling streams of water. He rode as far west as he intended. Normally, he would have ridden in a different direction to check on things but normally, he didn't have a young child with him. He reasoned it had been a long day for Kit and headed back to the cabin.

Before they reached the little clearing, he smelled meat cooking. His stomach growled.

Kit heard it. Maybe even felt it and he giggled.

Was there a better sound than a little boy enjoying life?

They went to the barn. He unsaddled then handed

Kit a curry brush and side by side, they brushed the horse. Luke murmured a few instructions.

Finished, they washed at the pump and then headed for the cabin.

The table was set. Honor greeted them with a smile. Luke could hardly wait to tell her about the day.

Kit pulled the little rock from his trouser and handed it to Honor.

"Why thank you. It's very pretty." She tucked it into her pocket.

Kit ducked his head but not before Luke saw the flare of pleasure in his eyes.

After supper, he and Kit helped with dishes then Kit got the book.

"You read?"

"Sure." It seemed a good way to spend the evening. Again, they sat together on the bed, and he read until his voice grew hoarse.

He smiled at Honor as Kit slept against her arm.

They settled him on the cot and slipped outside.

"He had quite the day." Luke relayed the events of the day. "What did you do?"

"I looked at his things in that old gunny sack. I suppose I should have asked him first." She scrubbed at her chin. "He doesn't have hardly anything. He'll need some clothes and shoes and—" She let out a long sigh. "Everythin'. I did find something interestin' though."

He raised his brows in silent question.

"A book. All words. I didn't understand any of them. But I left it."

They walked around the clearing, never far from the cabin in case Kit woke up. Not that Luke thought it would bother the boy to discover himself alone.

He laughed bringing Honor's curious gaze to him. "I was thinking how we're so careful to stay close to the cabin. It's not because we think Kit would be upset to see he was alone. It's because we don't want him to be alone."

She caught his arm and squeezed it. "I'm glad you feel that way too."

He pulled her into his arms. "He's like you, isn't he?"

She looked up at him. "In that, he doesn't have parents and has been left by the one person who might care for him, yes. But not in the most important way. He's with people who want him."

He hugged her. "Yes, he is and so are you now."

She rested against his chest.

Feeling tension in her, he rubbed her back. After a few minutes, her breath puffed out and she relaxed into him.

He had two people in his life that needed to know they could count on him and his love.

He might be a failure compared to Matt. For sure, he'd failed at a lot of things, but he did not mean to fail at this. With God's help, he would be everything they needed.

15

For the fourth day in a row, Honor waved goodbye to Luke and Kit. It was nice to see the two of them together. It was good for the boy. But it left her home alone and lonely.

There was so little she could do. Except think and her thoughts weren't always comforting. She and Luke had slept on the narrow cot since Kit had joined them. She enjoyed being close. Several times in the night she'd waken and turn to put her arm casually across his chest. She didn't know if he woke or acted in his sleep, but he always brought up a hand and covered her arm. For the first time in her life, she felt accepted. Maybe even loved. Though he'd never said those words.

Even if he never did, she was happy to be part of this new family.

And Kit. He was relaxing more and more every

day. She loved the boy so fiercely it squeezed her heart. She would do everything in her power to give him all the things she'd wanted as a child. Those things could be wrapped up in one word—love.

She pulled out the rock Kit had given her. Every day he brought her something. A rock. A handful of flowers. A bird nest. A big pinecone. She wasn't sure what it meant to him, but she cherished each gift.

They'd asked Kit about his belongings, and he'd taken everything from the gunny sack. His few items of clothing needed mending which gave her something to do.

Luke had looked at the book and said it wasn't English.

"It was Mama's," Kit whispered, his eyes wide.

Luke handed the book back to Kit. "When we go to Crow Crossing, we'll see if anyone can tell us what language it is."

It would give them a clue to his background. At present, they knew nothing but his first name and a guess as to his age.

The one thing she hadn't spoken to Kit about was his nightmare. It had only been that one time, so she let it go.

The next morning Kit didn't follow Luke to the door after breakfast.

Luke waited. "Are you coming?"

"I stay."

Honor couldn't keep back a wide smile. "I'd like that." Her smile flattened. Maybe Luke would mind.

He patted Kit on the head. "That's a good idea. You and Honor can do something together."

Kit kept his attention on his empty plate.

She caught his chin and lifted it. Waited until he brought his gaze to her. "I am very glad to have you keep me company today."

His mouth didn't smile but his eyes did.

They went to the door and waved goodbye to Luke. They remained on the threshold until he rode out of sight.

Kit followed Honor back to the table. He helped her gather up dishes and dried them as she washed them.

"How would it be if I make a lunch and we go to the river to eat it? I found berries down there." She hadn't gone up the hill for berries since Luke's warning. "We can take containers and pick some. Then I'll make a special dessert for Luke. What do you think?"

"It's a good idea." He was so solemn, but she saw the way his eyes brightened. It was enough to make her look forward to the outing even more than she already did.

She put slices of roast rabbit in the last of the breakfast biscuits and added a handful of cookies. It grew more challenging every day to bake with the limited supplies and to come up with a nourishing meal. Not that she minded. And Luke had never complained. It was only that she would have liked to do more and better.

She filled a little sack, and they headed out the door. The whole day stretched before them, theirs to enjoy. They took their time going to the river, climbing rocks, playing tag in the trees, and watching ants carrying loads far too big. It was time to eat by the time they arrived. They enjoyed the lunch and drank from the crystal-clear stream.

Remembering something she'd liked doing with the Johansen children, they lay on their backs in the grass and watched clouds.

"I see a bucking horse," she called.

She pointed out various things, wondering if Kit would play the game. "I see a snowman." His voice was whispery as if afraid to pretend.

She cheered. "I see it too."

But after a bit, the clouds turned to wispy broom tails. She sat up. "I need to pick berries if I'm going to make a dessert."

"I help." Together they made their way to the thicket. She guessed they were what she'd heard called serviceberries.

"I like berries." Kit's mouth and hands were purple.

Honor laughed. "I can see that." She looked at her stained hands. "Is my mouth as purple as yours?"

"Yup." His eyes sparkled.

Oh, how good it was to see the boy coming alive

and enjoying himself. He was a good-looking child with white-blond hair and bright blue eyes. And even better looking when he smiled. He'd improve even more when he filled out and she meant to see that he got fed well enough to do so.

Their containers held enough berries for her to use and they took them back to where they'd left the lunch sack.

"Now what?" She looked to Kit for a suggestion.

"We have to go back?"

"Not yet." The sun's position informed her she didn't have to rush home to make supper.

"What's over there?" He pointed across the river.

"Why I don't know. I've never gone over. You wanna go explore?"

He nodded.

"Guess we'll need to find a way across." The water was too deep to walk across without getting wet and it was cold.

"I show you."

"You found a bridge?"

He shook his head. "Follow me."

"Let's go." She chuckled at the way he grinned at her and followed him, wondering what he had in mind.

They went downstream a distance. They'd been almost this far when they explored on their arrival. She hadn't seen a bridge.

"There."

She couldn't tell what he meant.

"The rocks."

Then she understood. A row of rocks, some partly submerged, others sticking out of the water formed a series of steps that would allow them to cross. "It looks a little scary."

He scampered ahead and hopped from rock to rock as light-footed as a dancer. "Come on." He stood on the other side of the river beckoning to her.

"Well, if a six-year-old, skinny boy can do it," she muttered. "I can." She stepped to the first rock. It was wide and not scary. The next was narrower and she balanced. The third had water running over it. Looking at it made her feel dizzy. She swayed to retain her balance. Finally, she made it across but not without almost falling. Not once but twice.

And to think she had to go back that way. But she smiled at Kit. She would not let him know how hard she'd found the crossing.

A grove of trees shouldered to the side of the river and Kit caught her hand and dragged her forward.

"Birds. Listen."

They stood quiet and still until the birds started singing again then grinned at each other.

After a minute of enjoying the birdsong, they moved on. There was moss on the side of trees to examine, seedling trees growing from a dead stump to study, and mushrooms to consider. She might have picked some to add to their meal but had no idea if they were poisonous so left them. They reached the end of the bushes. She glanced at the sun.

"It's time to go home."

Kit led the way back through the trees to their rocky bridge.

She drew in a deep breath and pushed down her nervousness.

Kit began the crossing. Something in the water caught his attention and he squatted to look. He turned to report to her. "Little fishes."

The turn put him off balance.

"Careful." She held out a hand as if she could catch him.

He wavered, trying to right himself but his foot slipped, and he fell face-first into the cold water.

"Kit." The word screamed from her tight lungs. The water wasn't deep but deep enough that Kit's head was beneath the surface. "Kit." She stepped to the first rock. Careful. She needed to get to Kit, not fall in the river.

Kit was on his hands and knees.

"Kit, get up. Get yourself to the other side."

The boy pushed upward, staggered, and went down again. She realized the current pulled at him.

She hurried from rock to rock until she could lean down to grab him. "Kit, take my hand."

Kit tried again to stand and was pulled out of her reach.

She jumped into the water. The cold shocked her

but she ignored it. She grabbed Kit and dragged him to the bank. On dry land, she turned him to face her.

"Are you all right?"

"Cold."

"Yeah, me too." She hugged the boy as her heart settled back to its normal pace. "You scared me."

He pressed his head to her shoulder and leaned into her.

She held him another moment then pushed to her feet. "We need to get home and out of these wet things." Holding Kit's hand, she rushed back to where she'd left the lunch sack and berries. Shivering, they trotted toward the cabin.

Lord God, please don't let him get sick from this.

The cabin came into view. At the same time, Luke rode in from the other direction. What was he doing home so early? Had something gone wrong? But she didn't have time to stop and ask him.

The three of them reached the cabin at the same time.

Kit broke from her hold. "I'm sorry. I'm sorry." He sobbed brokenly as he ran inside.

Luke blinked. "What's going on?"

"He fell in the river."

Luke swung from his saddle and stared at the door through which Kit had disappeared. "Why is he so upset? Did you give him a whupping?"

"What?" Is that what he thought of her? "No, I did

not." Her voice grew sharp. "It seems you will always misjudge me."

She hurried after Kit. Her hands shook as she helped him out of his wet things, and it wasn't only from the cold.

* * *

Luke slapped his palm to his forehead. He hadn't meant to criticize Honor. But seeing them both soaking wet, their lips blue from cold had driven every reasonable thought from his head. He would explain himself to Honor, but she was no doubt changing out of her wet things.

He'd give her a few minutes.

In the meantime, he'd take care of his horse and he led it to the barn.

He watched, thinking Kit would join him. The boy came out, glanced toward the barn then went around the cabin and out of sight.

Luke sighed. He'd somehow failed the both of them despite his resolve not to do so.

He squared his shoulders. The day was not yet over. He finished with the horse and headed for the cabin. He rapped on the door. "Honor, can I come in?"

"Yes."

He entered. She stood facing the stove, her attention on a pot. She wore dry clothes. Her wet things and Kit's were missing. She must have slipped out to spread them on the bushes when he was busy with his horse.

He waited but she didn't so much as glance over her shoulder or offer a welcoming word.

"Honor, I didn't mean to question you about how you deal with the boy." That didn't exactly say what he meant, and he tried again. "It's just when I saw you wet and shivering..." He took two steps and closed the distance between them. "You both looked miserable. Then Kit raced away, saying he was sorry. I don't know." He scrubbed at the back of his neck. "I supposed he'd misbehaved. My pa didn't hesitate to whup us if we did." He shrugged. "I misspoke. I'm sorry." He waited. His heart refusing to push blood to his brain. What if she wouldn't forgive him?

"I seem to always be making a mistake." His words held a note of desperation.

"I guess we both make mistakes." She slowly came around to face him. Her gaze darted to the side as if looking to put more space between them. Then she brought her eyes to him. "I can see how you'd think he'd done something wrong. He didn't. And although I wouldn't hesitate to discipline him if I had to, a spanking would not be my first choice." Her eyes darkened to midnight blue. "My uncle was a little too free with the strap. I vowed I would never be like that."

He opened his arms.

She hesitated and then stepped into his embrace.

"We have much to learn about each other," he

murmured against her hair. "But I hope you know that any mistakes or blunders I make are not because I don't care. Like my pa said, I'm sometimes rash. I'm trying to fix that."

She chuckled softly. "Don't try too hard."

He grinned. "Thank you."

"Let's find Kit." But she didn't shift from his arms.

He didn't move either. "Why do you think he was so upset?"

She stepped back. "It's hard to know. Maybe Hob warned him he must never mess up or we might send him away."

He pressed his forehead to hers. "Honor, I hear years of hurt in your words. Let's be clear with each other and with Kit that we are committed to making this work 'til death do us part.'"

She lifted her face. "Thank you." Her smile could have moved mountains. It definitely eased the tightness around his heart.

He took her hand and together, they went in search of Kit.

The boy sat against the wall of the cabin, hunched over his drawn-up knees.

They joined him, one on either side.

Luke put his arm around the boy. His heart melted like butter when Honor pushed tightly to the boy, pressing Luke's arm to her shoulder.

"Kit, did you think I'd be angry with you?"

The boy sniffled and nodded.

"It was an accident. We all have accidents and make mistakes." He certainly had made his share. "I would never punish you for that."

Kit continued to study his knees.

Luke looked to Honor.

"Kit, honey, Luke promised that he will always be here for us. I promise the same thing. I will stay with you and Luke through thick and thin."

Luke held his breath in the pause following Honor's words. He hoped Kit would accept their promises. Perhaps even make one of his own though the child was young. Maybe too young to understand the value of a promise.

With a shuddering sigh, he lifted his head. "You want to keep me?"

"Yes." Luke and Honor spoke in unison. They smiled at each other though there was determination rather than amusement in their expressions.

"Even if I'm bad?" Kit whispered.

Luke smiled though it was an unspoken acknowledgment of how many times he failed. He guessed Honor's smile relayed the same message.

He shifted so he could look into Kit's face. "You need to understand that we all make mistakes. That doesn't mean we stop caring or give up on people." He caught the boy's chin. "Kit, I promise that I will never give up on you."

Kit's gaze clung to him for a long considering moment before he spoke. "I'll never give up on you either."

It was all Luke could do not to laugh. Then he sobered. No doubt he would need both Kit and Honor to stick with him.

Honor stood and pulled Kit to his feet. "Who wants supper?"

"I do." Luke rose and took Kit's other hand.

"Me too," Kit shouted.

The three of them laughed as they returned to the cabin.

Honor ground to a halt. "Wait. I don't have supper made." She pressed her palm to her forehead. "What am I going to do?"

Luke and Kit glanced at each other. Luke wondered if she was as worried as she seemed.

"Oh, I know." She faced them. "You two go out and find something to do while I get food ready."

Luke took Kit outside. "Best we wait out here."

"Why?"

Luke had meant it as a joke but saw the way Kit's forehead furrowed. "So we don't distract her. I wonder what she's going to make."

"Something with berries we picked."

"Berries? Where did you find them?" His heart jolted halfway up his chest.

"By the river."

His heart settled back into place. They hadn't gone where he'd seen the bear. "Umm. That sounds good."

Pots banging on the stove and something thudding on the table informed them Honor was hard at work.

"Let's go for a walk." He reasoned that time would pass faster if they did something.

Their steps slow, they walked up the trail that he rode every day. It was hard to believe they'd been there two weeks. And yet they'd packed so much into those two weeks.

Kit squatted down to watch a beetle crossing their path. "I don't think Honor would like him." He rose and looked around.

Luke understood he wanted to take something to Honor. Not only because he always did but because the three of them had crossed some kind of bridge.

He had an idea for something they could both give her.

16

Honor didn't consider herself a singer, but she couldn't help but sing a song of joy and thanksgiving. She and Luke had weathered another bad spot and come out the other side stronger and more certain of their marriage. They'd both made mistakes, and both had forgiven. It was a good way to be because like they'd said to Kit, they all make messed up at times.

She wanted to make the meal special, a celebration. But her options were limited. However, she would do the best she could. She stewed the fruit and made sweet dumplings. For the main part of the meal, she used the last of the rabbit stew she'd made yesterday. Thankfully, Luke kept them supplied with meat. She had no potatoes but there was a bag of rice and she added enough to thicken the stew. If only she had fresh vegetables.

Remembering how her aunt loved greens that someone picked in the wild and brought to her, and recalling she'd seen lamb's quarters behind the barn, she slipped out and picked the tender leaves.

She looked around but didn't see Luke and Kit. Had they gone for a walk? She hurried back to the kitchen. In a short time, the meal was ready. "Supper," she called from the door.

The pair trotted down the trail. They stopped when they saw her. Seems they carried a plant of some sort. What was that about?

She returned inside to stir the stew. The fruit and dumplings were done, and she moved that pot away from the heat.

Luke and Kit stood in the doorway.

Why did they both look—was it eager or guilty? She decided their bright eyes meant it was the former.

"We brought you something." Luke grinned at each other. "You get it, Kit."

He ducked behind Luke. Luke turned to help. They held a pail full of dirt and a seedling spruce tree.

She looked from one to the other. "What is this?"

"It's for you." Kit looked to Luke for assistance.

"It's to plant by our house back at the ranch. It will put down roots and grow tall and strong. Just as our family will."

Tears stung Honor's eyes as she realized the significance of what they'd brought her. "It's the best gift I've ever had. Thank you both."

They put the pail outside the door under her supervision.

"Thank you." She leaned over and gave Luke a gentle, quick kiss.

Kit watched them wide-eyed. Hungry eyed.

Honor bent over and kissed his forehead. "Thank you."

Kit shuffled, hiding his face but she knew he liked it. Knew he needed to know love. Just as she'd longed for it all her life.

Maybe she was now going to get it.

Supper was a celebration. Not because of the food even though that was good, but because of the tender feelings binding the three of them together.

It was later than usual by the time they cleaned up after the meal.

Kit got the book and handed it to Luke. As had become their habit, they sat together on the cot. Kit fell asleep almost immediately and Luke left off reading.

They slipped away from the boy and went outside, moving far enough away that their talk wouldn't disturb him.

"A tree was a good idea." She smiled up at him.

"I hope we will look at it and always remember this day."

She longed to ask what the day had meant to him but of course, he referred to their promise to Kit and each other though she and Luke had made the vows the day they married. But repeating them, especially after a disagreement, made them feel fresher and stronger.

She tried to hide a yawn, but her eyes watered with the effort.

"You're tired."

"Guess maybe I am." Between running through the trees chasing Kit and falling in the river, the day had taken its toll.

"Then let's go to bed." He caught her hand and hurried her indoors.

She lay on the bed, and he slipped in behind her. It was a tight fit. But comfortable. Was anything better than having Luke's arm across her and listening to Kit's slight snore beside her?

THEY SAT at the table the next morning, about to eat breakfast when Luke pushed to his feet. "Someone riding up."

Honor's heart leaped to her throat. She darted a look at Kit. Then silently pled with Luke. *If it's Hob, please don't let him take Kit.*

Luke nodded and she knew he understood and agreed. He looked out the door. "It's Shorty. One of our cowboys. He's got a loaded packhorse."

Honor released her breath in a whoosh and her heart settle back into place. Supplies were a good thing.

Air whistled from Kit's mouth. The poor child had worried about Hob too.

The cowboy stopped at the hitching rail and tied the horses.

"Come in for breakfast," Luke said.

"Don't mind if I do. I hoped I'd get here in time for some hot food."

Luke introduced Honor and Kit to the young man who sat on the end of the bench closest to Luke. Kit huddled close to Honor.

Luke asked the blessing, and the food was passed. Thank goodness she'd made plenty so there was enough for another hungry person.

The men lingered over coffee.

"Nice to see supplies." Luke drank from his cup.

"They're for me. Riley and the others sent me to take yer place. Seems to me they was some concerned for your soul if you missed goin' to church two Sundays in a row." Shorty chuckled, enjoying the look on Luke's face.

Luke snorted. "That sounds more like Matt."

Shorty shrugged. "Could be. I just do what I'm told." He drained his cup. "Best be on your way. It's a long ride back."

Luke set down his empty cup. "I'll pack up. Honor, can you make sure we have something for lunch?"

"I'll find something." Good thing she'd baked lots of biscuits for breakfast.

Shorty was on his feet. "I'll bring in the supplies. Might be something you can use."

Shorty had brought a large chunk of cheese. She took some for the three of them but left the bulk of it for him.

As soon as she'd prepared the lunch, she gathered up her things and Kit's. She considered sticking Luke's belongings into his saddlebags, but he returned before she could do so.

A few minutes later they set out. Luke led the two pack horses with the little tree—its roots wrapped in a gunny sack—hanging from one of them. Kit rode behind Luke.

She imagined the tree growing over the years then shifted her thoughts to the here and now. "Seems you have all the responsibility."

His eyebrows rose at her comment. "How so?"

"You have the extra horses and Kit. Maybe Kit could ride with me."

"I fine." The boy clutched at Luke and gave her a steady look.

She narrowed her eyes. "Are you saying you feel safer with him than with me?"

"No." He turned his face to Luke's back.

She laughed. "Yes, you are, you little scamp. Well, I don't blame you. He's a man you can count on."

Luke stared at her. "Do you mean that?"

"I wouldn't have said it if I didn't. Why do you look so surprised?"

He shrugged. "No reason." He turned his attention back to the trail.

Then it hit her. Her words were the opposite of those his father had said. She raised her voice to be heard over the distance, but she meant for him to hear each word. "I know I can count on you. It's a good feeling."

"Thanks." The smile he sent her way rewarded her.

They rode down the mountain, sometimes riding side by side, other times when the trail narrowed, she followed the pack animals They talked some but were content not to as well.

Honor liked knowing they were comfortable with each other.

When the sun was high in the sky, they stopped at a little stream to eat lunch and let the horses rest.

Kit wandered along the edge of the water, bending often to examine something.

Luke sprawled out beside Honor. "I wonder how he'll adjust to our big family at the ranch."

Our? She liked that. She gave his question some thought. "I think he'll be a little overwhelmed at first, but we'll be at his side. He knows he can count on us. He'll do fine."

She couldn't explain why she suddenly choked up and blinked back tears.

Luke sat up and pulled her to his side. "He reminds you of yourself, doesn't he?"

She cleared her throat. "I never felt I had anyone I could count on."

"You do now."

"I know."

He caught her chin to turn her to face him. "I will do my best for both you and Kit."

"I know." She leaned in for a gentle kiss.

He sighed. "I regret to say we can't linger here." He pulled her to her feet, called Kit and they resumed their journey.

It was evening before they rode up to the ranch. Riley met them at the barn. He gave Kit a surprised look then chuckled.

"You two work fast, I see."

Luke acknowledged the comment with a grin. "They're tired and hungry. Can I leave you the pack animals while I take them home?" He handed the lead rope to his brother. "I'll return to help as soon as I can."

They rode to Luke's house. And hers. And now Kit's as well.

Luke lowered Kit to the ground and then helped Honor to her feet. He held her as her legs protested.

"I'll be back shortly. Don't worry about supper. I can grab something at Matt's."

"We have to eat. You might as well join us." She fought a desire to catch his shirt front and hang on, keeping him close.

"Are you sure?"

"I wouldn't say it if I didn't mean it."

"Very well. But don't fuss."

He left the wrapped tree on the ground by the house and rode away, leaving her staring after him, wondering what he meant by fuss. It was her job to prepare his meals. Unable to explain his words, she took Kit inside and lit a fire in the stove. What could she make that would take limited time and energy? In the pantry, she discovered a basket of freshly-picked vegetables, a loaf of bread, and a jug of sweet milk sitting on the shelf. Someone had thought of them.

Gwen? Most likely. She'd have to thank the woman—her sister-in-law. It was time for Honor to become part of this family in every way possible and becoming friends with Gwen was one step in the process.

It took a few minutes to prepare the vegetables, but the soup was ready, the bread sliced, and the table set, but Luke hadn't returned.

She showed Kit around. She took him to the middle room. "This is where you'll sleep."

She went to the far room. "Luke sleeps here."

He stepped into the room, looked around, and seemed puzzled. "Where you sleep?"

"That's my room." She pointed to the room closest to the kitchen.

He squinted. "Mamas and papas sleep together."

"Not always."

"Always. That's why they get married." The look he gave her left no room for argument.

She shrugged. "Do you want me to help you put your things in the drawers?"

"I can do it." He took his gunny sack to the middle room and opened a drawer.

Seeing she wasn't needed, she looked out the window, watching for Luke. She smiled, her heart churned out warmth as she saw him striding down the path. But he turned aside.

Her blood slowed. Shouldn't he be in a hurry to get back to her… them?

Perhaps Matt had called out to him.

But it was Gwen who appeared and who touched his arm in a gentle, claiming way.

Jealousy was an ugly emotion. And one—she informed herself—she didn't need to entertain. Luke was her husband and had promised to be true to her as long as they both lived.

That was enough.

But she wanted more. She wanted to be loved and cherished. Even if she wasn't what he had asked for in his request for a mail-order bride.

He entered the house. "Supper smells good." He noticed the bread. "You didn't have time to bake."

"Someone left us a loaf."

"That would be Gwen." His gaze went in the direction of Matt's house even though the walls prevented him from seeing the other woman. "That's like her."

"It was kind of her." There was no reason to feel anything but gratitude for the gifts.

Seems her uncertainty about belonging would take time to get over.

* * *

"It was a good meal. Thanks." Luke patted his stomach. "It's good to be home too." He hadn't introduced Kit to the others yet though he'd stopped to tell Gwen, pleased when she put her hand on his arm and said she knew he'd make a great father.

It was on the tip of his tongue to say his usual teasing comment about her having chosen the wrong twin, but it seemed inappropriate in light of him now being married so he'd thanked Gwen for her vote of confidence and continued on his way.

"Well go to church with the others tomorrow. Gwen said to tell you that they have dinner planned for when we get back. So you don't have to prepare anything." He shifted his attention to Kit. "You'll meet my brothers, my twin brother's wife, their little girl, and Wally, who has worked here long enough he's almost the boss."

Kit's eyes grew round. "So many people." He waved his arms in a circle. "Big ranch."

"Remember we're all family. Your family now." Knowing Honor's feelings, he turned to her. "Yours too."

Kit and Honor grinned at each other as if sharing a

secret... one he knew. Family was something they'd never known.

He couldn't imagine. His brothers had always been there for him even when it was annoying.

He'd gotten into the habit of helping to clean the kitchen after the meal. He saw no reason not to continue doing so tonight.

They finished and he signaled the other two to follow him outside. "We need to put this poor little tree in the ground. Where should we plant it?"

Both he and Kit looked to Honor for her opinion.

She paced off several feet from the path. "We need to give it room to grow tall and wide." She stopped. "How's this?"

Luke carried the tree and the shovel to the spot. "Looks good to me." He dug a hole. Honor helped him position the tree. Kit brought a bucket of water and dumped it on the tree.

Luke reached for Honor and Kit's hands. "Every time we see this tree, let's think of how we are growing together as a family." The moment felt special. "Let's thank God." The three of them bowed their heads as he prayed. "Lord God of heaven and earth. You make plants to grow and see that it is good. You bring people together and it is very good."

Honor squeezed his hand to acknowledge she understood his reference.

He continued, "Thank you for bringing us together and making us a family. Amen."

They remained there a moment longer before heading for the house.

Luke would have liked to sit together again to read and reading as had become their habit, but Kit was falling asleep on his feet.

"Time for bed, young man."

Honor turned him toward his bedroom. "Get ready and I'll come tuck you in."

Kit looked from one to the other. "You not come?"

Luke silently consulted Honor. He would have liked to have a little time in the evening for just the two of them.

Their gazes held for a moment. Did he see reflected in her eyes the same longing he had?

She turned back to Kit. "I think it's nice that you have your own bedroom."

He shook his head, a stubborn look on his face. Though he saw uncertainty in the boy's eyes.

"I want to sleep with you like before."

Luke went to the window though he paid no attention to the scene. He didn't know how much more he could take of this sharing a bed with his wife like brother and sister.

Honor guided Kit toward his room. "Why don't you try it?"

She stayed to help him undress. Then signaled Luke to join them "Let's hear his prayers."

"I can pray?" Kit sounded surprised at the notion.

Luke shook his head. "I can see we have some

catching up to do. Of course, you can pray. Anyone can."

"Why?"

"You ask hard questions, but I'll do my best to give a good answer. God invites us to ask Him for what we need. And of course, we should thank Him for all the things He gives us."

Kit listened intently. "Like you and Honor?"

Luke chuckled. "Like you and Honor." He tapped his finger to Kit's chest and draped an arm across Honor's shoulders. "My mama taught me to pray before I can even remember."

Kit's bottom lip trembled. Before he could cry, Honor pulled him to her lap. "Maybe Luke can teach you like his mama did him. Would you like that?"

"Yes."

Luke stroked his chin thoughtfully. "I'll try and remember." A thousand forgotten memories flooded his mind. He didn't have time to dwell on them. "Ma always taught a little lesson before we prayed though I didn't think it was that at the time. I just liked her talking to me."

"That sounds nice," Honor said.

He guessed she was as eager to hear him repeat his ma's words as Kit and tried to bring a particular talk into focus. "I recall one time when Pa had taken Matt with him and left me behind because I hadn't finished my chores. Ma said I needed to listen to Pa. She quoted a Bible verse. I don't remember the words exactly, but I'll never forget the message. The verse said that wise sons listen to their father's instructions. Then she added: if we follow what the Bible says we'll never go wrong."

Kit's hungry eyes devoured every word.

Luke felt as if his mother looked over his shoulder with approval as he continued. *Thank you, Ma, for what you taught me.* "Let's kneel beside the bed."

The three of them knelt side by side, Kit in the middle.

"Praying is easy. You just talk to God. I'll show you. Dear God, our loving heavenly Father, we thank You for loving us, for keeping us safe, and for bringing us together. Forgive us for the wrongs we have done." Remembering how he'd misjudged Honor, he squeezed her shoulder.

She covered his hand with hers.

He continued, "Help us do what is right and good and help us have a good sleep. In Jesus' name, Amen."

Silence followed his words.

"Kit, do you want to pray?" He'd understand if the boy was hesitant.

"Yes. Dear God. I don't know much about You, but You made the world. Guess that means you made me and Honor and Luke. I'm glad we're now a family. Amen."

Luke was speechless at the boy's prayer. It was the most words he'd strung together since they found him on the doorstep.

"Was that good?" Kit asked.

Luke hugged the boy. "It was very good."

Honor added her arms to the hug. "Very good indeed. Now climb into bed."

Kit slipped under the covers. Honor pulled them up to his chin and leaned over to kiss his cheek. She stepped back to allow Luke to kiss him.

"Goodnight, son," he said as they left the room.

The two of them alone at last. They sat side by side on the couch. He stretched out his legs and let out a sigh of deep contentment. "It's good to be home."

"I hope Kit adjusts to all the changes."

Luke took her hand. "He'll do fine. After all, we're here for him."

She turned her palm to his.

"Having him here has made me remember so many things about my mother that I'd forgotten."

"I'm guessing good things from your tone."

"Yup. I recall Ma kneeling by her bed, unaware that I watched her. Or maybe she knew it and didn't mind." Picture after picture of his mother raced through his mind. "I see Ma reading her Bible in the evening and then her head bowed. I might have thought she slept but her lips moved silently, and I knew she prayed." He trailed off.

"What wonderful memories. You must miss her a lot."

"I do. I'm sorry you don't have the same kind of remembrances." His heart ached for her. "But from now on we'll create good memories. For Kit as well as us."

"I like that."

He pulled her close and dipped his head to hers.

She covered her mouth and tried to hide a yawn.

"You're tired and here I am keeping you up."

"I don't mind."

He didn't want the evening to end but they had many days ahead plus church tomorrow. He pulled her to her feet. "Time for bed." Would she invite him to her room?

She held his hand and drew him with her in that direction.

They stepped into her room. He took her in his arms. "Are you sure?"

She lowered her head then as he waited, looked up at him, her eyes dewy and inviting.

He caught her lips, gently at first then deepening the kiss.

A sound jerked him to attention.

"Kit, what's wrong?"

The boy's eyes were wide as twin moons.

"I sleep here. With you." He sounded so uncertain that Luke's heart went out to him.

Hadn't he just promised to give Kit as well as Honor, the kind of security he had grown up with and took for granted? He looked to Honor for her reaction.

Her gentle smile might have held a bit of regret. At least he let himself think so. "It's up to you."

She lay the decision entirely on him.

He sighed. What had Ma said about love? Putting another's needs before his own?

Sooner or later the boy would have to sleep in his own room. But it was only fair to give him a few days to adjust. "You can sleep here. Tonight."

Honor squeezed Luke's arm. "Our time will come."

"Promise?"

She smiled, her eyes flashing.

"I look forward to it."

Color flooded her cheeks making her freckles darker than normal and he chuckled to know she wanted to truly be man and wife.

17

Honor dressed carefully the next morning, wearing the sateen dress she'd come to despise because it was hot and uncomfortable, but she wanted to look her best for Luke.

Be honest. You want to look as good... if not better than Gwen.

She did her hair as close to how Tammy had taught her as she could. But there was nothing she could do to disguise her overabundance of freckles. She and Tammy had tried everything before Honor had finally decided she'd just have to accept them. "I suppose they're meant to keep me humble." Tammy had laughed at that. And Honor understood why. There was nothing in Honor's life that would give her reason to be proud.

That might have changed. She was now married to Luke Shannon.

She grinned at her reflection. Her freckles would always remind her not to think more highly of herself than she ought.

"Are you ready?" Luke called.

Smiling widely, she hurried from the room. Luke was resplendent in a white shirt and black jacket. She'd done her best for Kit but he had only his worn, too-small pants and an equally worn and small shirt. At least they were mended and clean. She must speak to Luke about the boy's needs.

Luke crooked his arm toward her. She rested her hand on his forearm. He held Kit's hand and they walked down the path to where the buggy stood in front of Matt's house.

Matt helped Gwen to the front seat and lifted Lindy up.

Luke introduced them to Kit then they got aboard and headed down the trail. The others, on horseback, waited to join them. Luke again introduced Kit. The boy said hello despite his shyness.

She hugged Kit. "I'm guessing you've never seen so many people at one time."

He nodded and sat back on the seat.

Lindy turned to study him. "How old are you? I'm four? Do you like cats? I have four in the barn. Cat and her three kittens. I can give you a kitten if you want. I have some hideouts in the trees. You wanna see them?" She finally paused to take a breath.

Kit stared at her opened mouth then murmured, "Yeah."

Gwen and Matt grinned at each other then she turned to smile at Luke. Was it an after-thought that she shifted enough to look at Honor. "She likes to talk."

Honor thought it seemed rather obvious, but it was nice to be included.

Lindy chattered to Kit the whole trip, a never-ending source of information. They heard more about the cats, about the garden, about how she played in the loft. She told about climbing a tree and not being able to get down. "Uncle Luke rescued me."

Honor wondered at the look Matt and Gwen exchanged but they reached town and she prepared herself for seeing others.

They parked and made their way into the church.

She let out a quick breath when they sat down. Kit between her and Luke. Luke and Matt beside each other. She settled back to enjoy the service. Luke opened the hymn book and followed the words as he sang. She looked at the page but couldn't read fast enough so could only sing the hymns she was familiar with.

The preacher spoke of God's faithfulness and Honor's soul was refreshed.

Pastor Ingram greeted them. Luke introduced Kit to the man. Then turned to the boy. "Would you go with Uncle Matt while Honor and I talk to the preacher?"

Kit reluctantly followed Matt, glancing back several times.

"I expect you wonder how we came to have a little boy so soon."

The pastor smiled at Luke's words. "It did cross my mind."

Luke explained the circumstances. "How would we go about adopting him?"

"I'm not sure, but I can make some inquiries if you like."

"I'd appreciate it."

He waited until they stepped away to speak to Honor. "I hope you don't mind that I didn't consult you about this, but I only thought of it when I got here."

"I am in total agreement."

His grin was wickedly teasing. "I guessed you would be. In fact," he leaned closer, "I was certain of it."

She laughed softly as they joined the others. Her delicious feeling lasted all the way back until they stopped in front of the bigger house. She'd almost persuaded herself to forget she was about to share the meal with the entire family.

Luke led her inside. "This is the house Ma and Pa built. We all lived here until recently. Pa insisted we all build our own houses."

She knew that from his letters. Knew too, that there were six bedrooms. *Small but each of us got our own bedroom and there was a spare room Pa thought Ma might need for guests or a woman to help her. That never happened.*

The long table in the kitchen was set. Wally and Gwen joined them each carrying a covered dish. Andy pulled something from the oven.

"What can I do?" Honor asked.

"Nothing, thanks." Gwen smiled. "We often eat together as a family after church. And it's a chance to welcome Kit."

Honor twisted her hands together, feeling awkward and out of place. She wasn't used to standing by while others did the work.

They gathered around the table. Riley asked the blessing and food was passed from hand to hand. For the most part, the conversation was about ranch business leaving her free to sit back and hope to be ignored.

Her desire was squashed when Gwen lifted a hand. "Enough about work. Let's talk of other things." She looked to Honor. "Tell us how you enjoyed being at one of the line shacks. I've never been to one myself."

"I liked it. There were berries to pick and places to explore."

"She made real good meals. Didn't she, Kit?" Luke said.

Kit looked as if surprised at being included. "Yeah," he murmured.

Gwen brought a big cake with fluffy icing and served them each a piece. Of course, Honor had never made anything like that cake. For one thing, the supplies in the line cabin didn't allow it. But she kept her observation to herself.

The food was gone, and Lindy was excused. She turned to Kit. "Wanna see the cats?"

Kit hesitated.

Luke squeezed the boy's shoulder. "Go ahead."

He got from his chair and followed Lindy out. Lindy a bubbling bundle of energy and non-stop talk, Kit was quiet and restrained.

Luke smiled at Honor as if reading her thoughts. Luke rested his arm on the back of Honor's chair.

The others seemed inclined to linger over coffee. Honor finally began to relax as the men teased each other. So, this is what having siblings would have been like.

She had missed out on so much.

A tiny sigh might have escaped because Luke's fingers pressed to her shoulder, and he gave her a look that clearly asked if something was wrong.

She smiled. His concern made everything right.

Finally, Riley stretched and yawned. "I might have a Sunday afternoon nap." It was the signal to end the gathering.

Honor's offer to help with dishes was dismissed. She thanked everyone for their welcome and the good meal and with Luke at her side, returned to their house. The afternoon passed pleasantly enough. They walked leisurely along the trail between the trees. After a quick supper, Luke read to them again. That evening, Kit again insisted on sleeping on the floor beside him.

Honor turned into Luke's arms. They'd agreed they'd wait until Kit chose to sleep in his own room, but she saw no reason they couldn't hold each other and kiss.

He held her tight in his arms as they fell asleep.

THE NEXT MORNING, he hurried out after breakfast to work on the horses, and she headed for the garden, Kit in her wake. He was soon bored and ran to play with Lindy when she called to him.

Honor smiled. It was good for the boy. He not only had her and Luke as parents, Luke's brothers as family but now he had a friend close to his own age.

Gwen joined her in the garden and said much the same to Honor.

The women worked side by side, sharing ideas on canning the vegetables and how to prepare for winter.

LIFE SETTLED INTO A ROUTINE. Meals to prepare. Garden produce to take care of. Laundry and mending. One day when the men were all away, Gwen suggested that she and Honor take the children on a picnic.

Honor readily agreed. She was growing more and more comfortable with Gwen's friendship.

They packed food into a sack and went a distance from the ranch. The children ran and played. Lindy shrieked at the fun while Kit chuckled quietly.

The women sat on the quilt watching the children.

Gwen shifted her attention to Honor. "How are you enjoying ranch life? It's quite a change from city living, isn't it?"

Honor chuckled. She was certain Gwen meant the primitiveness of the ranch in contrast to the luxury that existed in the homes of the rich residents of Kellom. Gwen didn't know that her home here was a palace compared to what she'd had back there and life was so much easier. Especially shared with Luke and Kit.

"I'd always wished I could move West."

"Is it all you hoped it would be?"

Honor adjusted the corner of the quilt beside her afraid if she looked directly at Gwen her expression would say so much more than her words. "It's more." She had a husband who vowed to be true to her and a little boy whom she loved.

"I have found it to my liking." Gwen leaned closer. "There's only one thing missing."

"There is?" Honor couldn't keep blurting out her surprise.

"School. But I've decided that this winter I'll start teaching Lindy her letters and numbers. Are you going to teach Kit?"

"I haven't thought of it." It was impossible for her to teach something she didn't know. But she couldn't admit it to Gwen.

Somehow, she'd learn how to read and write. She'd ask Luke to teach her.

* * *

LUKE FOUND married life most satisfactory. He enjoyed Honor's company and made sure to end his work early enough to spend an hour or more with her in the evening. He continued to read Robinson Crusoe to her and Kit. His only regret was that Kit still insisted he must sleep in their room. But he understood Kit's insecurity and was willing to wait.

On Sunday he'd realized the boy needed new clothes. He decided today was the day to take care of that business and at breakfast informed her they were going to town. "The three of us. When can you be ready?"

She jumped to her feet. "Now."

He laughed. "I have to get the wagon. Honor, can you please pack a lunch." Whistling merrily, he sauntered down the trail to the barn.

Matt eyed him up and down. "You're mighty happy."

"Guess so. Going to town. We need anything?" He meant for the ranch or for the others.

"You could ask Gwen. Or better yet, take her along."

He squinted at his brother. "I hope you're joshing because I'm only taking Kit and Honor."

Matt grinned. "So that's the way it is?"

"That's the way it is." He harnessed the horses and drove the wagon toward his house. Call him selfish if that's how Matt saw it but he had no intention of sharing his time with Honor with anyone else but Kit.

Kit waited for him and climbed into the wagon, but Honor waved him inside. Wondering what he wanted, he went to her.

"Can you address my envelope please?"

He considered her. "You know how to do it."

"I'm ashamed of my printing."

"Very well." He wrote Tammy's address, blotted the ink, and handed her the letter.

"Luke, I have one more request."

"Anything you want."

A smile flickered across her face. "Teach me to read and write?"

He squeezed her shoulders. "Of course." He kissed the top of her head.

They joined Kit and were on their way to town. Half an hour later, they pulled up in front of the store and went inside. Luckhams had a limited selection of boy's wear. The pants were too long but Honor said she would fix them.

Kit beamed as they completed their purchases and handed him the parcel.

They were about to leave when Luke remembered the display of books. He'd never paid attention to the children's selection but now he did and looked through them.

Mr. Luckham joined him. "The young lad might enjoy this primer."

"I'll take it." It wouldn't be only Kit who learned to read from it.

They stopped beside the trail for lunch on the way home.

It was a lovely way to spend the day.

He dropped Kit and Honor off at the house before he took the wagon to the barn. It was strangely quiet. Where was everyone? He finished tending the horses and still none of his brothers or Wally showed up. Not even Lindy. Was there something wrong?

* * *

Honor put away Kit's new clothes. For now, they'd be saved for church and going to town. She looked at the book Luke had bought. She knew her letters and could sound out most of the words. What she wanted to be able to do was read a grown-up book with big words. Once she could, she'd read the few words in the book about the west that had fueled her desire to move. And then she'd read the book Luke had given her. About Lewis and Clark, he'd said.

She prepared supper, but both Kit and Luke were missing.

Guessing she'd find Kit with Lindy and Luke at the barn, she set out to tell them the meal was ready.

She approached Gwen and Matt's house. Only the screen door blocked the entrance. She heard Luke's voice. Good, it would save her from going further for him.

She saw him through the door. Talking to Gwen. There was no sign of Matt. Luke's eyes had a look that she thought was for her alone. A claiming, wanting, tender look.

He loved Gwen. The knowledge blasted through her like an explosion.

Just as he loved Corine. Words of his letter to Mrs. Strong were suddenly clear—a woman such as my brother married—educated, refined, cheerful.

She had to escape, but she couldn't make her feet move.

"Here we are." Lindy's voice carried like a trumpet from behind Honor

Luke's gaze jerked to her. Surprised. Guilty.

"It's suppertime." She managed to get the words out without choking, then rushed home.

"Wait." Luke hurried after her, but she didn't stop until she was safely in the kitchen.

She crossed her arms and faced him. "You love her. You always want what Matt has. You always compare yourself to him. Can't you see you're just as good as he is? Just different. Isn't it all right to be different?" Thankfully, Kit still played with Lindy so he wouldn't overhear her. If only he would say being different is fine and her being different than Gwen was a good thing.

But he said nothing.

18

Luke stared at the food before him. It could have been slop for all it appealed to him. "I was only asking her where Matt and the others were. Seems a cowboy rode in to tell them there was some kind of mix up and they all needed to go help." He said nothing about her accusation that he wanted what Matt had.

Because he did.

For most of his life, he'd felt second best to his twin.

It sounded self-pitying to say it aloud. So, he didn't.

He choked down the food and left the table. "I have to do all the chores." He slipped away, welcoming the escape from the tension in the room.

Chores didn't take nearly enough time, so he spent an hour working with the colt. Dusk filled the shadows and darkened the path when he headed back.

Dread increased with each step. How was he to face her? Face the truth about himself?

The house was in front of him, but he shifted to the right, seeking his private trail.

Boys, never forget that God hears and answers prayer.

His mother's voice echoed loud and clear in his mind.

If only she was here, he'd seek her counsel.

But he knew what she'd say and what she'd advise. *Behold, thou desirest truth in the inward parts: and in the hidden part thou shalt make me to know wisdom.* It was a Bible verse she'd often quoted.

He wasn't sure he wanted to confess the truth.

He leaned his forehead on a tree. *God show me what to do. How to fix this.* His thoughts scurrying about like hungry mice. They began to slow and grow orderly.

Yes, he'd often felt second to Matt.

Yes, he'd wanted someone like Gwen. Hoping it would make him equal to his twin.

But it was Honor that he got. She'd been a surprise from the first time he saw her tripping on those silly shoes.

His heart lifted like a newly released bird set free from a snare. Happiness and joy bubbled upward, bringing a smile to his lips.

Every doubt, every regret vanished.

It was Honor that he wanted. He raised his head as those words edged through his mind.

Can't you see you're just as good as he is? Just different. Isn't it all right to be different?

Yes, it was all right to be different. He didn't mind being different so long as Honor liked what he was. And he certainly didn't mind that she was not Gwen.

How was he to convey that to Honor?

Truth. And trusting God.

He made his way back to the house knowing she might have already gone to bed. He stepped inside. The lamp burned low on the table. She sat waiting.

"Good, you're up."

"Yes, I need to talk to you." Her voice revealed weariness. Or was it wariness?

"Let me go first, please."

"Very well."

He pulled out the chair kitty-corner from her, wanting to be close yet not so near as to scare her away. "You're right. I've always felt second-best to Matt. He was born first. And I always felt Pa favored him. But talking to you these past few days has made me see that he treated us differently because we are different." He paused to consider his next words. "I told you I loved Corine even though she had given her heart to Matt. Then Gwen came. Maybe I thought I deserved Gwen."

"Or someone like her."

He flinched at the pain her voice revealed.

"I realize I was only trying to be Matt again.

Honor, I don't want to be Matt. I don't want what he has. I want to be me. I want what I have. You."

She ducked her head. "I can't read or write. I deceived you. And I have these awful freckles. How can you want me?"

He caught her hands. "Because you are exactly what I need and want. You complement me. You make me feel good about myself. You are perfect in every way."

She faced him, surprise slowly replaced by pleasure. "You mean it."

He recognized it wasn't a question. "Now and always." He pulled her to her feet. "Honor, I love you. Forever. I hope you can forgive me for being dumb and—"

She planted her fingers over his lips to silence him. "I love you, Luke Shannon. You and you alone.."

Their kiss lasted a long time. Then he pulled her to him.

She eased back enough to take his hand and lead him to their bedroom. "I have a surprise for you." She opened the door.

"Where's Kit?"

"In his own room. It seems Lindy told him only babies sleep with their mama and papa."

"He's no baby." He chuckled and drew her into the room.

Tonight, their love would be fulfilled, and their hearts forever bound together.

EPILOGUE

*L*uke helped Honor into the wagon as Kit jumped in the back.

He studied the boy. "Don't you look nice?" He wore sharp new clothes. His blond hair had been cut and combed back. He'd filled out.

"Today is special."

"It certainly is." They made their way to town and their meeting with the judge Pastor Ingram knew. He smiled at Honor, pressed to his side. "Every day is special," he whispered to her.

Her smile was like a kiss from heaven.

"Have I told you how much I love you?"

"Not since breakfast."

They laughed together, sobering as they approached town. As Kit said, today was a very important day.

Luke stopped the wagon in front of the church and

the three of them went inside. The pastor stood beside a man with a crown of silver hair.

Pastor Ingram introduced them to Judge Anson.

"First, let's deal with this." He returned to them the book Luke had sent to him in the hopes of learning more about Kit. "As far as I can learn, this is Norwegian."

"Is that his heritage?" Luke asked.

The judge studied Kit a moment. "It would explain his coloring. Unfortunately, there is nothing to provide a clue about his family."

Luke and Honor stood on either side of Kit and placed their hands on his shoulder.

"We are his family." Luke's words were firm. He and Honor had discussed this, and they'd had long talks with Kit. The boy was clear that he wanted to be legally theirs.

The judge pulled a sheaf of papers from his briefcase. "I have prepared legal adoption papers. Once you sign this you are the legal parents of this fine young fellow." He spoke directly to Kit. "Is this what you want?"

Kit nodded.

"I need to hear you say it."

Kit stood up tall and confident. "I want Uncle Luke and Aunt Honor to adopt me so I will always be their son."

Honor sniffed.

Luke's eyes stung and he blinked several times.

The judge spread out the papers. "You sign here, here, and here."

A few minutes later, he handed a copy of the papers to Luke, folded the others, and returned them to his briefcase.

"Congratulations. You are now father, mother, and son."

"My mama and papa," Kit said.

Honor and Luke hugged him.

They rode from town. They'd discussed what they should do for a celebration and agreed on a picnic for the three of them. They stopped at a grassy hill.

"It's where you brought me on my first day." Honor's eyes glistened.

He hoped she had only good memories of that day.

They spread out the picnic and he asked the blessing.

Honor smiled from Luke to Kit. "God saw the family He had created, and it was very good."

Luke's smile tugged at his lips. It must have rivaled the sun for brightness.

Life was indeed very good and he was certain there was more to come.

He leaned over to kiss Honor then settled back to enjoy the afternoon and the company of his dear wife and his new son.

ALSO BY LINDA FORD

Buffalo Gals of Bonners Ferry series
Glory and the Rawhide Preacher
Mandy and the Missouri Man
Joanna and the Footloose Cowboy

Circle A Cowboys series
Dillon
Mike
Noah
Adam
Sam
Pete
Austin

Romancing the West
Jake's Honor
Cash's Promise
Blaze's Hope
Levi's Blessing
A Heart's Yearning
A Heart's Blessing
A Heart's Delight

A Heart's Promise

Glory, Montana - the Preacher's Daughters

Loving a Rebel

A Love to Cherish

Renewing Love

A Love to Have and Hold

Glory, Montana - The Cowboys

Cowboy Father

Cowboy Groom

Cowboy Preacher

Glory, Montana - Frontier Brides

Rancher's Bride

Hunter's Bride

Christmas Bride

Wagon Train Romance series

Wagon Train Baby

Wagon Train Wedding

Wagon Train Matchmaker

Wagon Train Christmas

Renewed Love

Rescued Love

Reluctant Love

Redeemed Love

Dakota Brides series

Temporary Bride

Abandoned Bride

Second-Chance Bride

Reluctant Bride

Prairie Brides series

Lizzie

Maryelle

Irene

Grace

Wild Rose Country

Crane's Bride

Hannah's Dream

Chastity's Angel

Cowboy Bodyguard

Copyright © 2023 by Linda Ford

All rights reserved.

No part of this book may be reproduced in any form or by any electronic or mechanical means, including information storage and retrieval systems, without written permission from the author, except for the use of brief quotations in a book review.

Made in the USA
Monee, IL
05 March 2023